NANCY VIAU

BEAUTY AND Bernice

Schiffer Publishing Ltd®

4880 Lower Valley Road · Atglen, PA 19310

Other Schiffer Books by the Author:
Just One Thing!, ISBN: 978-0-7643-5162-4

Other Schiffer Books on Related Subjects:
A Promise Stitched in Time by Colleen Kosinski, ISBN: 978-0-7643-5554-7
The President and Me: John Adams and the Magic Bobblehead by Deborah Kalb, ISBN: 978-0-7643-5556-1

Designed by Brenda McCallum
Type set in FG Efficient/ Adobe Caslon/ Jokeman

ISBN: 978-0-7643-5580-6
Printed in China

Published by Schiffer Publishing, Ltd.
4880 Lower Valley Road
Atglen, PA 19310
Phone: (610) 593-1777; Fax: (610) 593-2002
E-mail: Info@schifferbooks.com
Web: www.schifferbooks.com

For our complete selection of fine books on this and related subjects, please visit our website at www.schifferbooks.com. You may also write for a free catalog.

Schiffer Publishing's titles are available at special discounts for bulk purchases for sales promotions or premiums. Special editions, including personalized covers, corporate imprints, and excerpts, can be created in large quantities for special needs. For more information, contact the publisher.

We are always looking for people to write books on new and related subjects. If you have an idea for a book, please contact us at proposals@schifferbooks.com.

To C-Bass, J-Bone,
RickyRoo,
and Dude—my gnarly
adventurers

CONTENTS

ACKNOWLEDGMENTS

A big thank you to those who helped me create this story—from editors, agents, and friends who read first drafts to those who offered suggestions for revision right up until the very end.

A special thanks to my family. Your support, encouragement, and patience means the world to me.

To the amazing, hard-working team at Schiffer Publishing, I appreciate *everything* you do.

And finally, a loving thank you to my wonderful parents, who had the best intentions when they sent me to charm school to polish my social graces. (See, Mom and Dad? I turned out just fine.)

Long, Long Ago in a Land Called Pennsylvania

My obsession with princesses was my mom's fault.

It started with an outfit she bought at the mall. Cinderella was my favorite fairy-tale character, and she thought it'd be sweet if Cindy and I matched. I couldn't have been more thrilled! I pranced around in that blue puff of satin fluff and told everybody—including the paper boy, the mail carrier, and the TV repair lady—that I was Cinderella and that I actually slept in the attic. I whistled at the birds, swept the carpet, and pretended that Butch, our dog, was my fairy godmother.

When it came time for preschool, I dressed in a jumper and an apron, transforming myself into a peasant girl. An imaginary beast was my princely friend, and I was destined to be his princess. I made sure my beast sat with me during snack and nap time, and I got very angry when the teachers ignored him. Cranky Mrs. Higgins told my parents I was a difficult child, and that I'd be better off in another school.

Every night I'd slip into my mermaid princess bathing suit, and splash in the tub until my fingers and toes were raisins. I felt that if I stayed in there long enough, I'd grow a tail—a glistening green-and-purple tail, complete with fins. Dad let me have my way until his patience went down the drain, and he airlifted me into a towel, kicking and screaming.

I felt a special connection to all princesses. I had no doubt that I, Bernice Baransky, would grow up to be exactly like them—beautiful and charming. I would marry a prince. I would live in a castle. And I would live happily ever after.

But that was then.

This is now.

Now, I'm twelve. Practically a grownup. I'm not beautiful or charming, and I'm totally over the princess thing. So, I have to wonder: *Why is there a princess hanging out in my yard, and why does she have her shiny silver slipper planted on my skateboard?*

Three Time's the Charm

Truth is, I have a pretty good idea who this princess is. Three days ago, while I was cruising around on my skateboard, I saw her drive by in a pink convertible. Usually, I don't notice the traffic that zips past me. I'm a sidewalk skater, thanks to Mom's rule about street skating. But a pink convertible is hard to miss! My first thought was: *Cars come in pink?* My second thought was: *Who IS that?*

A girl about my age, maybe a year or two older, sat on top of the convertible's backseat. She wore a ridiculous gown that swirled around her in a cloud of fuchsia. Sitting on her golden hair was a tiara, and its jewels sparkled in the sun, practically blinding me. Her lacy gloves went clear up to her armpits, and she waved enthusiastically, like a beauty queen in a parade. I resisted waving back. Skaters don't wave. To anyone. Her car disappeared around the bend and I was left with an open mouth, wide eyes, and a brain full of questions.

Two days ago, the rest of the parade showed up—a humongous moving van with the words CASTLE AND COMPANY painted on the side, a double-wide horse trailer complete with a double-wide horse, four big cars, and a white designer SUV. The pink car brought up the rear and the same girl was in the back, only this time she had on a blue gown and a queen-size frown. I copied that frown the second the parade parked in the driveway of the old Miller mansion across the street. I wasn't in love with the idea that a princess look-alike was moving across the street from me.

An old woman climbed out of the SUV and gave me the once-over. To avoid her eyes, I quickly bent down and tied and retied my sneaks, twice. Then I turned to bolt for my front door. Just before I went inside, I heard, "Hello! Hellooo, Bernice."

It was not an old woman's voice. This voice was clear and musical. It had to be coming from the princess. I turned and sure enough, it was Princess Pink Car.

"You are Bernice, are you not?" she asked, flashing a toothy smile.

I had no idea how she knew my name. I didn't answer, but instead ducked inside and spied on her from the window in my door. She waited there for a second with one hand on a hip, then she glided gracefully into the mansion.

When I was little, a princess sighting would not have been a big deal. She would've been imaginary—the result of my overactive imagination. I probably would have asked if she wanted to join me for a tea party. But I was older and wiser now. A better explanation was necessary.

I decided I was smack dab in the middle of a brain fart. A brain fart makes your brain numb and nothing makes sense, according to Matthew, a kid from school. And so, I explained away my princess neighbor as a big, fat brain fart. No princess arrived in a pink convertible. No princess moved in across the street from me. No princess called me by name. Brain. Fart.

I held on to my brain fart theory until today. Today, the princess is here, standing two feet from me. She seems real enough, and I'm sure brain farts don't last three days. She's checking out my skateboard, using her glossy slipper to push it forward and back. She hasn't noticed that I'm standing here, staring. She hasn't noticed that I am not smiling.

I take in her shiny hair—blonde like mine only straight, less frizzy, and *way* nicer. Her perfectly plucked eyebrows arch over rose-colored eyelids. Her eyes are blue. Her cheeks are peachy. She's wearing a light-pink gown with a matching tiara.

Part of me—that teeny part that has never outgrown princesses—wants to know all about her. The other part wants to hold on to brain farts. I rub my eyes and blink a long, hard blink. Dang. She's still there! I wrack my muddled brain for something to say. One of us is crazy, and you can't have a conversation with crazy. I stumble backwards and attempt to leave.

The princess touches my shoulder. "Oh, Bernice! Hello, again!"

I turn to face her, and gulp out a weak, "Hi."

The princess sighs, steps away from my skateboard, and comes closer. She's only an inch taller than me. She presses her palms together and says in a formal voice, "Careful. Young ladies should walk with grace."

With *what*? I can't be hearing straight. Whether she's real or not, I can tell by the way she's bossing me around that she's already a royal pain in my butt. I want to tell her to get lost. I want to shout loudly and obnoxiously that I am not "young lady" material. I am a semi-fearless and often unladylike skateboarder, and I walk just fine. But before I get out a single word, she sashays her silver-slippered self home. I didn't get the chance to defend myself. Not that I would out loud, anyway.

I kick a stone off the driveway and watch it sail in her direction. Then I shimmy my ungraceful self through my back door.

In the kitchen, I find Mom busy in the walk-in pantry. Dad built her a mini craft room in there. She's seated at a long table that Dad made out of a plywood door. Canned soup, fruit, pasta, and other stuff lurk in the background. It's the beginning of July, but she's making a Christmas wreathe that she'll sell at the Porchtown Craft Fair in December. "Come on, work with me," Mom yells at a roll of red ribbon. "Get your act together. I may have to use brute force to get you tied nice and neat. I kid you not."

Mom talks to herself. Or to ribbons, pine clippings, colored straw, dried flowers, glue sticks, and any other material she uses to create the craft of the day. Dad says she's quirky and pretends it doesn't happen as often as it does. He'd love her even if she talked to animals on a regular basis.

"Um, Mom?" I say. "Did you happen to notice a prin—"

"Bernice! I'm glad you're here. Pinch this piece of ribbon so I can retie it. It's not cooperating with me."

I pinch and decide this is the perfect mother-daughter moment to tell Mom that either, one, we've got a crazy neighbor, or two, I'm the crazy one and my warped, brain-fart-filled mind has produced a princess in our backyard. Mom listens and doesn't once hint that I should be committed to the local loony bin, which I appreciate. One of the perks of having a quirky mom. I'm also not surprised when Mom's reaction to my situation is, "Maybe you and she can be friends."

That's when I realize the glue's finally gone to her head.

Mom is wrong.

The princess and I won't be friends.

There's not a skater on the planet who wants a princess for a friend. Seriously.

The Princess and the Plan

I haven't thought about princesses, read about princesses, or talked to imaginary princesses since third grade. By the time a kid reaches a certain age, it's no longer cool to be into princesses. I learned this the hard way via a prissy princess named Kylie Brooks. Kylie showed up in Ms. Light's class with an angelic face—one perfectly proportioned to her long neck, petite body, and cute feet. No one could walk past her without coming under her spell. I *had* to meet her. "Hi," I said. "Has anyone ever told you that you look like Snow White?"

Kylie didn't take that well. "Snow White?" she asked, tilting her button nose in the air. "What are you, like five years old?"

Her comment made my toes curl. I turned six shades of pink and pushed back a drippy tear that threatened to slide down my cheek. My best friend stepped in to save me. "Hey, Kylie," Roxanne said. "Bernie only meant that you look unreal."

Kylie smirked, not sure whether Roxanne had complimented her or made fun of her.

Then Roxanne yanked me aside and whispered, "What are you doing? We're too old for princesses."

Somewhere between that day and today, I changed my obsession from princesses to skateboarding. I got interested in skating after stumbling on the X Games on TV one Sunday afternoon. I had to try some of those tricks! Dad got me a cheap skateboard at Sports Mart and there was no turning back. Now, every chance I get, I pop ollies, ride the ramps, and practice tricks at the Porchtown Skate Park. Any birthday bucks or bits of cash have gone into equipment, like a cooler helmet or a better board. Given the choice between new clothes, new music, or shiny skateboard trucks—the metal pieces that attach to my deck and help my board steer—well, it's not even a choice.

The board I ride, an Optical Ellipse, is six months old. It's almost worn out already. I want a custom skateboard, one where I pick out the deck, the trucks, the wheels—everything, and Porchtown Sports puts it together for me.

For the last week, I've been weeding gardens to earn money for that new skateboard. That's why I'm here in our neighbor's garden. Mrs. Martin pays me five dollars an hour to get rid of onion grass, dandelions, and other stuff that smothers her precious perennials. I don't mind. This job is better than Roxanne's. She's a babysitter and there's no way I'm watching somebody's smelly kid. I have a hard enough time keeping *myself* injury free and smelling decent.

"Poor Bernice, must you toil the day away in the dirt?"

I don't have to look up. I know it's the princess. A chill works its way up my spine because her voice reminds me of the high-pitched violin music you hear in the dentist's office while they're scraping the living daylights out of your teeth. I stand and turn to face my new neighbor. "Toil? What? What are you talking about? And how do you know my name?"

The princess chuckles. "What a silly-willy you are." A singing sparrow appears out of nowhere and lands on her shoulder. Seriously. A sparrow.

"Who—"

The princess holds her fingers to her lips to shush me. She whispers, "My godmother, Serena, told me your name. She sent me to officially meet you." The bird pecks at her perfect hair. "I think that the salesperson who sold us the mansion told her about the people on this street, including you." The princess sweeps open her arms as if she's a queen waiting for her servants' attention. In a flash, her royal expression takes a hike, and she says, "One day I was napping in the woods of our beautiful European estate, and the next I was told we had to move here—Station Street, USA. Our new property lacks both acreage and a view."

A smirk sneaks out. "Let me guess, you're Sleeping Beauty and Serena is your fairy godmother?"

"No, I'm *not* Sleeping Beauty," the princess says, irritated. "But I *do* love that story, and I am, of course, a princess. My name is Odelia, and Serena is not a fairy, but she is my godmother. I've lived with her since my parents died." Odelia then turns to me with a curious stare.

I chew on my lip. It crosses my mind that I should bow or kiss her hand or something. Or maybe say that I feel sort of sorry for her. But down deep, I'm stuck for words. Mostly, I feel sorry that she's a freak who dresses like a fairy-tale character.

I take in the whole princess picture. Odelia's twisted bun looks as if it's from a hair magazine that advertises fancy up-dos. Her sparkling tiara sits squarely on that bun. Odelia's complexion is milky. No zits have ever planted roots there. Her nose is the ideal size and shape for her face. Not scrawny and slightly bent, like mine. And she has a Barbie doll shape—again, the opposite of mine, which resembles Barbie only from the ankles down.

"Are you for real?" I poke her shoulder. "You feel real."

"What an odd question." Odelia presses her lips together. "Yes, Bernice. I am real. And please, don't let me keep you from your household chores. Is there a mean stepmother in your life who makes you weed gardens?"

"No, I have a nice mom. What I'm doing here . . ." I pause and yank up a stubborn dandelion, "is not dreadful. It's something I do to help out my neighbor, and she pays me. I bet *you* wouldn't be caught dead doing *any* kind of job." I pound the dirt with my garden shovel and don't look up at Odelia. I can't believe I'm having this awkward conversation.

"Don't assume things about me!" Odelia says. She takes a big breath. "*I do* have a job—one that is better explained as a royal responsibility. If I do what's expected of me, I'll earn the respect of my godmother and be rightfully rewarded."

I shade my eyes from the sun and gaze up at the princess. Her chin is tilted ever so slightly upward, like she's so much better than me. "A royal responsibility?" I ask. "I'm not buying it. What exactly is 'expected' of you?"

"Haven't you figured it out, Bernice?"

"Nope," I say. "Not a clue."

Odelia sighs. "I'm expected to befriend you."

I'm pretty sure I'm the only kid who comes with a neighbor who has to be my friend because of a royal proclamation. "You've got to be kidding. How old are you, anyway?"

"I am thirteen," Odelia answers. "And one-half." She picks at her manicured nails, as if our conversation is a total waste of her time.

"You act much older."

Odelia twirls a strand of hair that has escaped from her bun. "I don't know how to act any other way."

"If you're a princess, there must be a prince around here somewhere. Is there?" I ask.

Odelia's peachy cheeks turn apple red. She studies her reflection in her shiny slippers. "Yes, there is a prince nearby. He moved here shortly after we did. But I don't want to talk about Prince Chancellor Pomegranate."

"Chancellor Pomegranate?" I say, giggling. "You're kidding! That's a ridiculous name!"

Odelia scoffs. "Do you have a prince?"

"Of course not!" But Wyatt, a cute skater I've seen at the park, crosses my mind. He's totally prince material.

Odelia raises her left eyebrow, keeping the right one glued in place. "Don't be rude, Bernice. You would benefit from what I know of the social graces."

"What?" I ask, copying her tricky eyebrow thing, hoping she'll laugh off the princess act, tell me this has all been a joke, and suddenly be normal.

"Everyone should be aware of the basic social graces—appropriate hygiene, posture, manners, etc." Odelia's face is stone. She's dead serious.

I need to get away from this weirdo. I back away, and go over to the shed to dump the garden tools. Inside it's cool and damp. My head is swimming, probably from hanging out in the hot sun for the last two hours. Thinking about Odelia, I've decided she must've camped out in the hot sun her entire life.

As I lock up the shed, I say, "I'm going home now."

But the garden is empty. Odelia's gone.

The Pied Piper and the Pipe

The last couple of days I've gardened my butt off, and Mrs. Martin's gardens are finally done. My wallet is twenty-five dollars heavier, and once I get cleaned up, I'm heading to my favorite hangout—the skate park, a few blocks away. Once upon a time, a group of high school kids successfully petitioned the Parks and Recreation Council to build the Porchtown Skate Park in two of the three unused tennis courts. Mom didn't let me skate there by myself until this summer. After a couple of years practicing in my driveway on plywood junk, I couldn't wait to try out the ramps, rails, bowls, and quarter-pipe. And they've added an eight-foot half-pipe in the third unused tennis court. So scary. You can bail on every other trick in the park, but once you drop in on that thing, you're going nowhere but down. My goal is to get up enough nerve to try it before the summer's over. Maybe even land a trick on it.

I change out of my muddy shirt and put on a fresh tee shirt. It's not exactly fresh. I wore it twice this week. No need for a shower because in fifteen minutes the stink I have on now will be replaced with an even stinkier stink. I tuck my wayward curls inside my beanie, then rip off the stringy threads that dangle from the sweat pants I cut off last week. They'll annoy me when I'm flying down the ramps. After tightening the laces on my favorite checkered skater shoes, I grab my gear, and go out the front door. I'm about to take off when I spot Odelia. She's hustling and bustling in my direction. If my skateboard had rocket boosters, I'd be halfway to Mars.

"Bernice! Where are you going?"

I check up and down my street to make sure no one sees me with a prom queen in July. Odelia's gown is midnight-blue today and although it's extremely beautiful—*she is* extremely beautiful—I will lose whatever sketchy bit of coolness I have if I'm seen i

"You should answer when someone as

"I'm going away from you," I mumbl

"Speak up, Bernice. Don't mumble-ju

"Skate park," I tell her.

"A park?" Odelia asks. "Is this plac
young men be there? Shouldn't you put

I ignore most of her questions bec
you're right. I almost forgot. I *do* need

"Yes, accessorize, Bernice! That's a good ...
occasion. Make the most of what you have. You have the potentia ...
more than rather plain."

"More than rather plain?" I repeat. I may be a little ordinary, but I've
never felt bad about that. Until now. I hide my hurt by making a big deal
out of sticking on my knee and elbow pads. I shove the silver helmet over
my beanie and give her an I-don't-care-what-you-think-of-me look.

Odelia's enthusiasm over my "accessories" fades. "You look like a knight,"
she says. "Please tell me you're not training for battle."

"What I'm battling is a brand-new half-pipe." I hold up my skateboard
and sway it back and forth like a heavy sword. "A skate park is a place with
ramps, pads, steps, rails, and other awesome obstacles. I ride this skateboard
up and down and over everything, and my 'accessories' are so I don't get
hurt when I mess up. And I mess up a lot. But I will own that pipe today."

"Own a pipe? Smoking? No, no, no!" Odelia shouts.

I blow out a sigh. "No, Odelia. I don't smoke. A half-pipe is a big U,
like a ramp with sides. It's got an insane vert, a *vertical*, and scares the
goosebumps off me, but I hope to be able to ride my skateboard on it by
the time summer is over."

Odelia smiles, enough that her dimples make an appearance. I can't
tell if she's been trying to fool me or she's serious.

"Lead on, warrior skater Bernice."

"You're coming?"

"Yes!" Odelia answers. "I am gathering notes on how to turn you, a
knight, into a lady. Onward!"

Why I don't tell Odelia then and there to get lost, I. Have. No. Idea.
Maybe I *do* feel sorry for her, being an orphan and the new kid in town.

Odelia strolls behind me, placing one foot purposefully in front of the
other. She's so slow that the sparrow following her has trouble staying in
the air. At this rate, she'll catch up to me next week. I hop off my board

p it up and down with my left foot. Odelia turns her
e jog, then she stops short, says, "Oopsies," and returns to
t. When she's near me, I start skating again, barely moving
keep my wheels turning and staying slightly ahead of her. I hope
thinks we are actually hanging out. I thank my lucky stars that
Street is deserted.

When we stop at the gate, Odelia touches my skateboard, then pulls
her hand away like it's an object from outer space. "Skateboarding is not
popular where I come from," she says. "Can you tell me about it? How do
you stay stuck to it?"

I answer Odelia's million questions about skating. She's so interested,
I wonder if she wants to try it. But a skater in a princess gown is about as
cool as a tutu-ed ballerina defending a hockey goal. She's not getting
anywhere near my board inside the skate park. Showing up here with a
royal sidekick is bad enough.

Lucky for me, the park is empty except for a few third-graders. They
whisper and point to Odelia, then get back to grinding the flat bar at the
back of the park. These shortie shredders mastered their first ollies when
they were seven. They come here every day, easily popping their boards on
to ledges, rails, and benches without a second thought. They let nothing
get in the way of a day of skating. Not even a princess spectator.

Today, it's burning hot out—like eighty-plus degrees with eighty
percent humidity, so the usual crowd isn't here. They've traded in their
skate gear for swimsuits and gone to the pool next door. I can't go swimming.
We don't have a membership. Mom and Dad say, "We're too mellow for
a pool membership," which is parental code for it's an unnecessary expense.
They encourage me to run through our sprinklers for fun. I may as well sit
on the front lawn with the word DORK on my swimsuit.

Odelia doesn't follow me into the fenced part of the park. She takes a
seat on the bleachers outside. She smoothes her gown, adjusts the periwinkle
ribbon that's around her waist, and dusts off her slippers with a lacy
handkerchief she's taken from her purse. Once settled—as settled as a
princess can be at a skate park—her eyes find me and stick to me like fresh
grip tape on a skateboard deck.

It's going to be a long day.

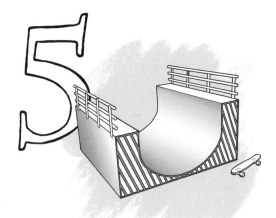

One Day My Prince Will Come

I roll around the park, pop an ollie, and end up on the manny pad—a four-by-six low slab of rectangular concrete. I practice my kick turns and pull off a couple of 50-50 grinds on the low rail. As I ride, I ask myself: *Is Odelia going to follow me everywhere? How did I get so lucky to be stuck with the town crazy person? Why does she have to be my friend? Why can't she be friends with Marcia Garcia, the ten-year-old on our street who walks around with a crown and a wand? They'd make a great pair.*

The third-graders have left and the regulars show up. These boys enter from the pool side and are too wrapped up in challenging each other with skateboard tricks to notice me or Odelia. At this park, in my corner of rural Pennsylvania, boys rule. I'm one of two girls in the entire town who show up here, but that counts for squat. Shiloh Brown, the other girl, is a beast at skating. She nails every move and gets lots of attention. I've learned a ton by watching her and copying her style. But Shi's gone for the rest of the summer, visiting her old neighborhood in San Diego.

I cruise over to the half-pipe. From ground level, this U doesn't seem that high. I pick up my board and run to the top. Different story from here. It's got to be as big as one of Bob Burnquist's mega-ramps! Maybe not, but the short, straight vert that hangs under my feet makes me dizzy. What am I doing up here? Maybe *I'm* the crazy one.

Sweat soaks through my gloves and the butterflies in my stomach have turned into blood-sucking vampire bats. I bite my lower lip as I balance on the coping—the straight, hard ridge at the top—and hope for the guts to take my board and my body over the edge. Odelia waves to me like a prom queen on a float, and I get distracted. No one saw that, right?

Moron Forge (known as Ron to his parents and to me because I'm too chicken to call him Moron to his face) yells, "Stop hoggin' the pipe, Berndog!" Moron is a loud-mouthed loser. He's not that good at skating, only at ordering everybody around.

Boys tie my tongue in knots, so a snappy comeback to Moron is out of the question. I send him a dirty look and back up that look with a killer move. I put my foot on the front of my board and WHOOSH! I launch myself off the top. Dropping in I feel an adrenaline rush—an outrageous rush that sadly lasts only a split second. As I lean back into the curve, I realize my mistake. I should have leaned *into* it. My board goes left. I head right . . . and . . . CRASH! "Yee OW!" I slide five feet across the plywood and land at the bottom. I end up crumpled in a ball like a discarded gum wrapper. Not pretty.

I do a quick body check to make sure I haven't cracked my spine. No bones are sticking out anywhere, so that's a plus. A blur of a boy runs toward me and when I finally focus, I feel faint. It's Wyatt. Wyatt Anderson. My insides turn to mush.

"Yo, that was epic, Dude. You alive?" he asks.

Wyatt has called me Dude since June 25th, the first day he rolled into the park on his black-and-red board. Wyatt obviously knows I'm not a boy. I have *boobilage*—insignificant chest pimples that I swear weren't there last month. I can't come close to getting mad at Wyatt for calling me Dude because I am in deep like with him. So deep in like with him that I can't form more than a word or two if he's within twenty feet.

News flash! Wyatt Anderson, the park's cutest boy, is hovering over me, talking to me. I stare into his chin and stall. I want to say something. Anything. I want to sound witty and smart. I want to pretend my leg is broken in three places, so he'll pick me up and carry me home.

"Dude, you got a concussion?"

I nod. "I'm good," I say, popping to a stand. I walk to the gate, trying to look all casual, when really my leg is about to amputate itself. I don't turn, but sense Wyatt's eyes burning into me. When I hit the corner, I limp like a clown on stilts, minus one stilt.

Odelia glides to my side.

I limp faster.

"Bernice," she says, annoyed. "Why do you go out in public looking and smelling like you do?" Odelia takes in an exaggerated breath, leans toward me, and pinches her nose.

I'm caught off guard and step back. A chill works its way up my neck.

Odelia taps her chin with her fingertip, and clicks her tongue. "And then you suffer the consequences because you can't muster up the confidence to talk to a boy. It's serendipitous that this has happened! I know now how to begin your instruction in the social graces."

"Seren—what?" Maybe Wyatt's right. Maybe I'm smack dab in the middle of a concussion.

"Ser-en-dip-i-tous," Odelia says, sounding out the syllables like a second-grade teacher. "It means an accidental discovery of that which is useful."

"Useful like a clean half-pipe run?" I snap.

"What I mean is that I've accidentally discovered—"

I interrupt. "The only thing you've discovered is that I choke up when I'm around Wyatt. I can't spit out more than two words."

"That's right!" Odelia answers brightly. "My social graces lessons will help you with that."

"Get this through your tiara-ed head, Odelia," I say tapping her forehead. "I don't want lessons of any kind, and I don't need your help. Even if you could help me, I can't be seen hanging out with someone who dresses as weirdly as you do. I'm a butthead for even letting you tag along today. I have to go." I let my board fall to the sidewalk, hop on, and push off toward home.

Beauty and the Butthead

I nod to Mom, who's sitting on the porch next door with her friend from the Handy Women of America Club. Dad's not home. He's slaving away at the family business—Jersey Bait and Tackle—that's over the state line in New Jersey. I have the house to myself, and that's a good thing. My parents won't question me about the gash on my thigh. They don't have a problem with me skating, but if they knew my little injury was the result of riding the half-pipe, they'd freak.

I put a glob of antibiotic ointment on my cut, but leave off bandages. Wimps wear those. And I am not a wimp. Truth is, I am totally a wimp. A wimp when it comes to talking to boys, but that doesn't count.

I head for the kitchen in search of munchies. I need to snack away my pain. Not the pain from the cut, the pain in my gut caused by that embarrassing moment with Wyatt. I had a boy's undivided attention, and I couldn't talk to him. He must think I'm a stuck-up idiot.

I could use some chocolate. There's no sign of a candy bar, chocolate chip granola bar, or fudge brownie anywhere in the pantry. I know Mom has stashed some goodies somewhere. I yank open the freezer door. A bag of chocolate sandwich cookies sticks out from underneath the frozen corn. Yay!

Standing over the kitchen sink, I gobble up five cookies, and when I look out the window, I see Odelia. Odelia, who insists on being my friend. She's twirling around, whistling a tune I don't recognize. The sparrow flits above her as she scribbles in a hot-pink notebook. I blink to make sure I'm not watching a scene from a movie.

My cell vibrates. It's Roxanne, but I don't answer because I'm not in a great mood, and I don't want to hear about her latest fight with her mom. Plus, I'm feeling slightly guilty about how I treated Odelia today. I got mad at her, but I was really only mad at my own awkward self. Since it's tough to ignore a princess bouncing around your yard, I push open the screen door and go outside.

"I'm writing down helpful hints," Odelia says.

"Hints?" I ask, peeking at the gold lettering on Odelia's spiral notebook:

ODELIA'S GUIDE TO THE SOCIAL GRACES

And when she turns a page, I look a little harder at what she's written inside:

LESSON 1: SQUEAKY CLEAN

OBJECTIVE: Bernice will learn the importance of hygiene. (Note to self: Bernice's current hygiene equals that of Penelope Pig, a runt I owned who had a fondness for malodorous bonnets and manure baths.)

I'm not sure what malodorous means, but it has the word odor in it, so it can't be good. It's the manure part that worries me most.

Odelia takes both my hands, squeezes them, and says, "Let's get started!"

"Started on what? Look, Odelia, these hints, or lessons, or whatever you're calling them—well, I don't care about them. Even if you think it's your royal responsibility to be my friend, it's not your job to clean me up."

Odelia picks at the edge of her notebook. "I . . . I want to help," she stammers. "If you let me, you'll soon be able to woo Wyatt."

"English, please," I demand. "What's woo?"

"You'll be able to talk to that boy at the park. You may even be able to impress him."

I let down my guard a little. "How would I go about that exactly?"

"By smoothing your rough edges and becoming more confident," Odelia answers smugly. "I've had oodles of practice with this since becoming a prin—" Odelia stops. "Since *I am* such a polished princess. Maybe with my help, you'll get what you want."

"I want Wyatt to think of me as more than just another skater, and definitely more than a dude." There, I said it out loud.

"If you work on your social graces, that might happen," Odelia promises.

"But I like skating and hanging around boys. Boys never worry about fashion, make-up, combed hair, or malodorous whatever. They only worry about mastering the next trick. Wyatt is one of those boys. He doesn't care how I look. He doesn't care how I *smell*. Does he?"

"He cares," Odelia answers, blowing out a huge sigh.

I plop on my swing. "When he ran over to check on me, it was like he expected me to say more; be more. Be more what?"

Odelia grins. "Be nicer, maybe?"

I twist the swing around, then lift my feet off the ground and let it spin me. If Wyatt sees me as a cool girl, maybe I'll fit in at Porchtown Middle come fall. Maybe I'll have a shot at being popular. "Wait. A. Minute," I tell Odelia. "You are not turning me into you, are you?"

"Of course not," she says.

"I will not give up skating."

Odelia sighs. "I understand."

I unravel myself from the swing. The next word that comes out of my mouth is a surprise, even to me. "Deal."

"Hooray!" Odelia shouts. "Serena will be so pleased. She thinks I've led a reclusive life. I haven't had many friends. We're officially friends now, right, Bernice?"

"I wouldn't go that far," I say.

Odelia ignores me. In a forceful voice, she reads what she's written in that pinker than pink notebook:

"ODELIA'S GUIDE TO THE SOCIAL GRACES

LESSON 1: SQUEAKY CLEAN

OBJECTIVE: Bernice will learn the importance of hygiene. (Note to self: Bernice's current hygiene equals that of Penelope Pig, a runt I owned who had a fondness for malodorous bonnets and manure baths.)"

Odelia scribbles something else in the notebook. Then she says, "And chocolate."

"Your pig didn't eat chocolate. You made that up."

Odelia doesn't own up to the truth but instead points to my mouth. I run my tongue over my teeth and taste the gooey chocolate mush that's stuck between each tooth. "I don't have pig teeth. And I don't smell as bad as manure." I lift up my arm and smell my pits. I could be wrong. It's pretty gross under there. "And what about the bonnet thing? I don't wear a smelly hat."

Odelia makes a sneak attack on my beanie. "Now, you don't," she says.

"Hey!" I squeal. "That beanie is my signature!"

Odelia throws the beanie on the ground. "From the tip of your nose to the soles of your feet, you should smell as fresh as a field of flowers."

"I am *not* wearing perfume."

"A light, flowery or fruity scent might do wonders."

"That's crap. I smell fine."

Odelia shoots that left eyebrow up and scribbles furiously. "What's that word, crap?" she asks. "It sounds awful."

Now I know for sure that Odelia has been living under a rock. "Crap is what you say when you're mad. It's sort of like a swear word, but not a bad one." When I listen to myself say this, I hear Mom and Dad in my head, scolding me for swearing. And crap is a word I'm never supposed to use.

"What does it mean?" Odelia asks.

"Well . . . it actually means poop."

Odelia's mouth drops open. She has the same horrified expression as Roxanne had when we saw parts of that old movie *The Exorcist*.

I try to explain. "All the kids say it."

"Fiddlesticks!" Odelia shouts, loud enough to send her sparrow away for good.

Odelia can yell? That's a surprise. She coughs and composes herself. "From this day on, say fiddlesticks instead. Please don't ever, *ever* say that awful word."

I feel small, like I do when Mom hollers at me. "What in the world is a fiddlestick?" I ask.

"It is a bow to a fiddle, silly."

"Fiddlesticks is a stupid word. I can't say that," I tell Odelia, jabbing her shoulder to make my point. Odelia brushes off my fingers. I can't help but notice how her neatly manicured nails clash with my dirty ones. And that she smells *way* better than I do.

Bubble, Bubble, Toil, and Trouble

I need today to be normal. I need today to be free of pushy princesses and skateboarding boys. I call Roxanne and tell her I'm dying for an icy. An ice-cold treat will remind me of what summer is all about. Roxanne's meeting me at Winnie's Icy Igloo after church.

Winnie's is owned by my aunt, Winnifred Haggerty. It's around the corner from my house, a short skateboard ride away, and it's on Mom's list of places I'm allowed to go on my own.

Roxanne and I scan the flavors listed next to the window to see if anything's new. Aunt Winnie asks me how my summer's going, what's been happening at home, how's Mom, and if Dad has caught any prize-winning fish lately. I answer and we order. I always get something fruity—a cherry one this time, and Roxanne samples two new flavors before ordering her usual—vanilla. We pick up our treats, walk to the side of the building, and lean against a shady wall. I chat about what I've been up to, skipping the fact that I've gotten sucked into makeover madness by the local lunatic. Roxanne complains about her mom. As usual.

"My mom has another audition set up for me tomorrow," she says, gritting her teeth. Roxanne's world is coming to an end. News at eleven.

"Just go. It can't be that bad," I assure her.

"I don't want to be in a dumb TV commercial. Let alone one for acne."

"You don't have acne. You've never even had a pimple."

"Duh. My mother won't let that stop her. She'll probably draw some killer zits on me and pray they'll pass for real ones." Roxanne sticks her finger into my cup. She dots her face with chips of red ice.

"Perfect," I say, and we laugh so hard that icy stuff almost oozes out of our noses.

I get a cup of water and Roxanne dips a napkin in it and wipes her face. "My mom's planning a fall-in-love-with-the-Big-Apple mini vacation. She's constantly reminding me that New York City is the place to be. After my audition, we're staying up there for a couple days."

"Maybe you can check out the beauty schools. You still want to be Roxy, Super Stylist to the Stars, don't you?"

Roxanne twirls a piece of her long, black hair. "Absolutely," she answers. "I've got skills. Take that girl over there, the blond-haired one with the braided ballerina bun that's stretching her forehead into next week. I'd change her look completely. I'd add auburn highlights, give her a chin-length bob, and oh *puh-lease*. Please tell me that is Not. A. Tiara. What normal person wears a tiara? And don't even get me started on her clothes."

I find the girl that Roxanne is talking about. I knew it. It *is* Odelia! She doesn't have on a princess gown, but it's close. It's a gold jumper tied at the waist with red-and-green plaid ribbon. Underneath she has on a bright white shirt with a lace collar. She sticks out like a marigold in a field of weeds. I gulp and send her a silent message: *Don't come over here. Don't let anybody see that we know each other. Please, please, please.*

A brown van pulls up and blocks my view of Odelia. Four boys in matching baseball uniforms pile out the sliding door. Boy number five has long legs and a lanky body. Wyatt! There's a slight lift of a pointer finger in my direction, and I imagine he's thinking, *Yo, don't I know you?*

My cheeks burn. I'm sure they match my cherry icy. I don't wave. Skaters don't wave. To anyone. Instead, I look down at my cup and smash what's left there with a straw.

"Who is *that*?" Roxanne asks.

I shrug. I don't want to let on that I know his full name. That he's never seen without a baseball hat that he wears frontward when drinking his orange energy drink and backward when he's sweaty. And that he rocks a front nose manual, a tough trick that involves riding on the front two wheels of a board. Oh, and that he doesn't know my name, but calls me Dude.

Roxanne nudges me. "Did he just wave to us? I wonder if he comes here every day after practice."

More intense icy-smashing on my part.

Roxanne walks her perky self around to the front window and pretends to read the flavors again. Wyatt and his team are seated a few feet away. When she returns, she pulls me in close and whispers, "I want to meet that boy and come this fall when we're in middle school, I want to ask him to the first dance. I've been praying for somebody to come into my dull life. My prayers have been answered."

I nod and drink the rest of my half-frozen treat too fast, giving myself a brain freeze. Even a headache doesn't take away the fact that there are things I should tell Roxanne. Like how I get to see this boy every time I'm at the park. He's *always* there. I couldn't miss him if I tried. Roxanne hates the skate park and never wants to come with me. But if I tell her Wyatt's a skater, she'll start showing up. And I want to keep him to myself, even if . . . well, I don't have the guts to actually talk to him.

"The heat's getting to me," I mutter. "I need to chill in the AC for a while. I'll catch you when you get back from New York."

"I should go, too," Roxanne says. "I'm babysitting this afternoon. But after my New York trip, this is what we're going to do: every chance we can, we'll come here." She checks her cell for the time. "Especially around one o'clock."

I don't need a full-out explanation to get where Roxanne's coming from. "It's Sunday," I remind her. "He probably has a different ball schedule during the week."

Roxanne shrugs. "So, we'll show up here as often as we can." She takes off, making sure to pass by Wyatt. She tosses him a flirty smile. At least, I think it was a flirty smile.

I walk home and try not to notice that Odelia is ten feet behind me, taking notes.

"Today's lesson is about poise," she says. "The objective is—"

"For you to get lost," I say. "I took a shower yesterday. *And* this morning. I'll smell ya later." I check Odelia's face to see if she has gotten my joke. She's not smiling.

Odelia stomps around and plants herself in front of me, shaking a finger like a gym teacher on a mission. "Your stubbornness will get you nowhere. I thought—"

"I'm going home," I interrupt. "Alone." I push past and hop on my board. When I'm three blocks away, I turn to make sure she's not leaping after me like a wild pony. She's gone, and I'm glad. I know she's disappointed, but I am not in the mood today to be Odelia's work-in-progress.

I don't go to the skate park, but I do ride around town. A warm summer breeze filters through my helmet, and my hair flies out behind me. I like how it feels and remember it was Odelia's idea to ditch my beanie. I figure I can live with this change. I'm not so sure about the other stuff she has in store for me.

Mom and Dad are in the living room when I come in. They're huddled together on the couch sharing parental secrets, but from my spot in the kitchen, I can see and hear plenty.

"Don't give me the hairy eyeball, George," Mom says. "It's not like I don't want to tell her. It's a difficult situation. The time is never right. It might change her. I love her the way she is."

Dad takes Mom's hands in his. "Hon, we can help her get through it. Let's tell her."

"Tell her," I chime in, stepping out from the kitchen.

Mom and Dad look up at me like they're surprised I live here. They scoot to the edge of the couch.

"Tell her the truth," I offer. "She'll listen."

I know what the big secret is. They're going on and on about Aunt Winnie behind her back. Aunt Winnie's been substituting treats and ice cream for a balanced diet for decades and weighs close to 300 pounds. Mom's been trying to get her to sign up for one of those TV reality shows that force you to lose weight.

"The truth?" Dad spits out.

"Tell Aunt Winnie she's overweight. It'll probably save her life."

"Oh," Mom and Dad say. Together they sink back into the couch cushions.

In the back of my mind, I think about how I didn't tell Roxanne about Wyatt. I feel kind of funny about that. But Roxanne won't end up in the hospital if Wyatt doesn't notice her.

"Yes, yes, you're right, sweetie," Mom answers. "I'll call Winnie, get everything out in the open."

Dad's wringing his hands. "Ellie, we never should have put this off for so long," he says. He sure is coming down hard on Mom for having a sister who doesn't eat right.

As I go to leave, Mom pulls me in for a random hug. I wiggle out of her grip, and she hands me a basket of clean laundry to carry upstairs. She reaches for her needlepoint project and begins yakking away at her supplies. "Come on, needles and threads, you have a date with lilies and primroses, and I have a date with the telephone." When I'm halfway up the stairs, she calls, "Bernie, I forgot to tell you that Mrs. Martin called. She told me she won't need your gardening skills for a while. A persistent salesgirl came to the house and sold them a swimming pool and a hot tub. Isn't that lovely? Lois has been bugging Bud for years for a pool and a tub, and all it took was a princess with a pitch."

"Princess with a pitch?" I ask, not sure I heard her right.

"That's how Lois explained it. The pool company is called Princess Spa. Their salespeople dress up like princesses. Who can resist a princess?" Mom continues. "Anywho, their entire yard will be a disaster for weeks. When the pool builders are finished and the new landscaping is in, they'll give you a call. I hope we'll be invited to a hot tub party. What a bubbly good time that will be!"

That princess couldn't possibly be Odelia, could it? But come to think of it, she was irritated that I weeded gardens. Maybe getting our neighbor to dig up her yard and install a pool was Odelia's way of taking my job from me. How far will she go to get me all to herself? I have a sneaky suspicion it's pretty far. And that makes *me* bubble a lot!

8
Practically Not Perfect in Every Way

Odelia's not giving up on me anytime soon. I know this because the very next day she's waiting outside my bedroom, dressed in purple princess gear from tiara to toe, pink notebook in hand.

"Who let the princess in?" I ask.

"Your back door was unlocked. I wandered in here by myself."

"I'm on my way out," I tell Odelia. "And I. Have. Showered. Aren't you thrilled?"

"I am thrilled!" Odelia says, gliding past me and parking her bustled butt on my bed. She sits there, straight and tall, picking at the corner of her notebook. "I wasn't sure I wanted to see you after your rudeness yesterday. But Serena insists I try harder to be a good neighbor."

Odelia shrugs one shoulder and the rod that's holding up her back bends a bit. She dabs a teary eye with a tissue she's fished out from her sleeve.

This poor girl is desperate to be my friend. I've decided not to ask if she was the one who showed up at Mr. and Mrs. Martin's house pretending to be a salesgirl for Princess Spa. It doesn't matter. I can let that go.

When I don't say anything, Odelia continues, a little perkier than before. "I told Serena I wanted to show you some of what I know about the social graces, and she was delighted. She told me, 'Odelia, you've embarked on a responsible, altruistic endeavor befitting a queen.'"

When Odelia imitates Serena, she's actually funny. I raise an eyebrow. "Let me get a dictionary because I can't understand what you're saying. I mean, what *Serena* is saying."

"Serena is happy I'm doing something for you," Odelia says. "And that we're doing something together. Can we try another lesson?"

"Do we have to?" I whine. "I was heading for the park."

"The hours are ticking by. Every hour you waste sends you further from your goal."

"Impressing Wyatt?"

"Yes. And you're on your way. You smell much better! Like cherry blossoms."

"It's scented body lotion. I smell like fruit salad."

"I'm pleased that you put lesson one into action. That lesson on cleanliness went rather smoothly."

"*Rah*-ther," I say, copying her.

"Only mocking birds mock. Be nice, Bernice." Odelia turns and takes stock of what's in my room. "Where might I find a . . ?" She doesn't finish the question, but asks a different one. "Who are these messy girls in this painting?"

"You mean on the poster? It's a band. They're called No Boys Allowed. They play locally. They're my favorite band, but they aren't famous yet."

"Why are they banging on metal objects?"

"It's a *percussion* band. They use trashcan lids, buckets, brooms, and other junk to make music."

"They look like they *are* trash. If I meet them, I'll be sure and share a few tips. Ah, that leads me to today's lesson." Odelia opens her notebook, and reads:

"ODELIA'S GUIDE TO THE SOCIAL GRACES

LESSON 2: POSITIVELY POISED

OBJECTIVE: Bernice will learn to be presentable and proud. Like an artist with a rough canvas, I'll create a masterpiece. (Note to self: Bernice has the poise of a tipped cow.)"

"Tipped cow! Really? *You* be nice, Odelia." I couldn't resist.

She giggles, and I do, too. It's nice to see that she can lighten up.

"No one talks about poise these days," I say. "I don't even know what you're talking about."

"Poise is elegance. It's a manner of presenting yourself neatly, with confidence."

I fall back on my bed and look up at the ceiling. "Whatever."

Odelia checks her appearance in my mirror, then looks at me. "We need to work on getting rid of your disheveled look."

"I told you, I showered." I get up and hold my armpit to Odelia's nose so she can get a whiff.

Odelia yanks my arm down and pulls me toward my dresser mirror. "Your hair is a bee's nest," she says. "It's time to get the bees out of the hive."

Odelia finds my hairbrush and starts attacking the knots in my tight, frizzy curls.

"OW!" I scream. "Is this necessary? If you keep this up, I'll be bald! Crrr—"

Odelia gently places the brush bristles over my mouth.

"Fiddlesticks!" I spit out. "This is a waste of precious skating time!" I grab the brush and throw it on the bed. "I'm outta here! I don't need this. I may not ever be impressive. I may not ever fit in at Porchtown Middle. But I'll just have to deal with it. I'm fine."

I start for the door, but Odelia beats me to it. She's a skinny wimp, yet somehow this skinny wimp has succeeded in blocking the door handle. She may be an inch taller than me, but I can take her if I try.

"Yes, Bernice, you *are* fine. And I *was* fine, too. That is, until I moved here from Europe. I wish I was back in my old home, in my old country. I'd be strolling through a grassy maze on my estate instead of here in this stupid place, fighting with you."

"Whoa! Where did *that* come from?"

Odelia rushes away from me. "Oh, I'm so sorry. That was mean. I've been in a foul mood. Please forgive me." Odelia holds her face in her hands and sobs like a lost toddler.

"It's okay," I say, handing her a tissue. "I didn't mean to yell at you. Everybody suffers from a brain fart now and then."

"Brain fart?" Odelia asks, sniffling.

I explain brain farts, and suddenly, Odelia bursts out laughing.

When I think about it, a brain fart is an immature idea, and I laugh, too. I'll be in middle school in a month and a half, so I better stop sounding like I stepped off the *elementary* school playground. I pick up my brush, and hand it to Odelia. "My hair could be neater, I guess."

Odelia attacks my hair again, but her touch is a little softer. "Think of me as a gardener who will remove knotty weeds and leave a better you."

Like that will ever happen.

Odelia brushes my hair for half an hour. It's shinier than it's ever been, and she's swept my bangs to the side. It's very seventh grade. She gives me a manicure and a pedicure and although uncomfortable in more ways than I can mention, the result is . . . well, interesting. I got her to substitute midnight blue polish for the disgusting coral pink she picked out, and for the first time in my life, every nail is identical in size, shape, and color. Very cool! I slouch in front of the mirror, arms across my chest, and strike a pose like the rappers do at the end of a song. My dark nails go with my black, ripped tee, the one with Kelly Slater surfing a humongous wave. And with my gray sweatpants pushed up to my knees and my tan high-top sneakers, which are more mud-stained than tan, I look tough. Like I could take on any skater in the park. "Not bad," I say.

"In the future, we'll discuss your clothing," Odelia says.

"In the future, we will not," I snap.

Odelia ignores me. "Lesson two is now complete. Let's move on to lesson three. Follow me to the lawn! We have lots to do!"

Odelia does not stop yakking the whole way. She's going on and on about good posture and how it affects my everyday life. I find this really hard to believe, but I listen anyway. Out of the blue, she starts talking about trees. I don't have a clue what she means until I hear the new entry in her notebook:

"ODELIA'S GUIDE TO THE SOCIAL GRACES

LESSON 3: BE A PINE TREE, NEVER A WILLOW

OBJECTIVE: Bernice will learn to position her body in
perfect balance in all aspects of her physical life. Perfect balance begins
with exceptional posture. (Note to self: Bernice's current posture
resembles that of the Hunchback of Notre Dame.)"

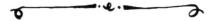

I point to the Hunchback part. "Did you *really* need to write *that*?" I ask.

Odelia chuckles. "I was trying to be funny, Bernice. Anyway, to my knowledge, this lesson always follows the previous one on poise. It involves maintaining balance while standing tall and—"

"Wait. A. Minute. I already have balance. You've seen me skate. I can't handle the half-pipe yet, but only a couple of kids can." I raise my voice. "I don't need this stupid lesson. Let's skip it. Let's skip *everything*. I'm going to the park."

Odelia pouts. "Fine. I'll tell Serena that it is not possible for us to be friends because you are impossible." She starts to walk away, but then turns around and practically shouts, "You are a big baby who doesn't want to grow up or change in any way. And if you stay the way you are, Bernice, you'll never be able to talk to boys. So, good luck. And good-riddance." Odelia pitches her nose to the clouds and stomps home.

Now who's the baby?

But Odelia's rant hit a nerve. I *can* be impossible. It's mostly because I'm not sure how to say what I want to say, what I *need* to say. Odelia has promised to help me, and I suppose I should let her. Plus, if she's bent on fulfilling some responsibility to her godmother—the responsibility that involves being my friend—I probably shouldn't mess with that.

"Odelia," I call. "Come back."

The princess turns. "Are you sure?" she asks.

For the next hour, Odelia keeps me busier than busy. She finds a bunch of Dad's fishing books in the garage and puts two on my head. I'm supposed to parade up and down my driveway without letting them fall. This is a lot harder to do than it looks. I tip. Books tip. We start over. Persistent Princess Odelia doesn't give me a break. "Straighten up. Pull your shoulders back," she says, more demanding than the bossy woman from that reality show with the models. "Look in the distance, not down. Carry yourself with pride. Show the world that you are strong and noble. You are a pine tree reaching for the sun in a shady forest. Walk tall. Toes forward, not out. Chin up, Bernice. Chin UP!" A drill sergeant in the army could take lessons from Odelia.

"I'm trying!" I yell. "It doesn't feel natural."

Odelia scowls. "People will judge you based on how you present yourself. Good posture shows that you have confidence. With confidence you'll achieve your goals. If you had confidence on that hill you call a pipe, you would not have failed."

"It's a half-pipe, and that's not true," I tell Odelia. "Posture doesn't count. In skateboarding or anywhere. You should be yourself. Only stuck up girly girls walk with sticks up their butts. I am not, and never will be, a girly girl!"

Odelia ignores my outburst. "This is the last exercise for today. Take this hefty book and balance it on your head." She shoves the *Encyclopedia of Saltwater Tackle*—all 743 pages of it—into my hands. I do what Odelia says, but not without a huge groan. In my mind, I say every single swear word I'm never allowed to say out loud.

After five tries, I finally get the book to settle on a flat spot—the new, smooth spot created by Odelia's expert taming of my wild curls. With my arms stretched out to my sides, I feel her laying a rolled-up boating chart on each bend of an elbow. In each palm, she drops a tennis ball.

"Walk," Odelia says.

And I walk.

I hate to admit it, but doing this reminds me of my happy princess days—those days when I was little and acting like a proper princess was everything to me. But I definitely don't want to go down that road again. What I really hope for now is that I come away with some skills I can take to middle school. And, although I'll never say this out loud, aside from skating, I've got nothing else to do this summer. Roxanne is my only friend, and she's constantly skipping off to New York. I'm not good at making new friends. The Kylie fiasco ruined that for me. But if I figure out how to fit in and still be cool, I won't have to work at finding friends. They'll find me.

Maybe Odelia and I *can* be a team. Especially if no one else discovers what we're up to. But Odelia's got to lose the gown and the tiara and the royal attitude, or kids will talk. I don't want to be known as Bernice Baransky, the kid who comes with a princess. I'll get eaten alive.

I make it to the end of the driveway and hear an old Madonna song blasting from a stereo. I catch Big Bubba—Dad's clunker of a pickup truck—turning in. Oh, no! Dad will see Odelia! And that's when the book, charts, and balls fall.

"Fiddlesticks!"

Awesome Is as Awesome Does

Dad steps out of the truck and comes running. "You cool-o-roonie, Bern?"

I turn and Odelia is nowhere in sight. I tell Dad, "I'm fine."

That was close. If Dad had seen Odelia, I'd have to come up with an explanation as to who she is, why she dresses like she does, and what in the world I'm doing hanging out with her. Ugh. Too much.

Dad picks up his charts and rerolls them. "Should I ask?"

"Nope. You wouldn't understand."

"If I didn't know better, I'd say you're practicing to become a model."

"No way," I say. "I'm not even close to model material."

"Miss Teen America?" he asks. "Are you entering a pageant?"

"Really, Dad?" I say impatiently. "I'd never do that."

"My cutie-patootie, whether you see it or not, you are a beauty. If you entered a contest, you'd be a shoe-in for first place. I've got other books in the basement, if you need them. And three old fishing poles. I've got cinder blocks, too. You're welcome to use those, if you want to build up muscle." Dad flexes his bicep. At least, I think that was his bicep. Hard to tell.

Dad's just being nice. "Let it go," I say. "Don't worry. Everything's good."

I look around to see if Odelia's hiding in the bushes, but she's not. All this time, I've been worried about how embarrassing it is for me to be seen with Odelia. And now it's just sinking in. She knows I'm embarrassed! I feel sort of bad about that. I suppose I could've introduced her as a friend—a friend who dresses like a princess because she's in community theater, maybe. Wait. Hold up for a minute. Odelia is a friend?

"Bernie," Mom hollers from the back door. "Can you come here?"

"Go rescue your mother," Dad says. "Her crafts aren't cooperating, and she's been hootin' and hollerin' at them. Poor gal's been frustrated with her progress since I left at six this morning, and she's phoned me twice to tell me about it. She's ready to send for reinforcements, like the ladies from her club or the needlepoint police." Dad winks and shoves me toward the door. "I'll clean up this mess."

Mom's Love's Fresh Lemon perfume scent hits me when I'm within three feet of her. Lemon is such a Mom smell. It's her signature fragrance. I consider my old signature—sweat, body odor, and board wax, and wonder if people will notice anything different now that I've discovered fruity body products. Mom is yakking on and on about Mrs. Martin. I tune in, hoping she's found a job for me like washing windows or cleaning out their garage. I need money for a new board!

"Since you aren't gardening anymore," Mom says, "I have an idea. At the Handy Women of America Club meeting, Barb O'Malley asked me if you'd like to help out at the summer camp her daughter, Nellie, goes to."

"Smile Academy? The camp for kids with Down syndrome?" I ask.

"That's the one. The counselors could use some help Tuesday and Thursday mornings, especially at craft time."

"Do I have to? This is a job for you, not me."

Mom opens the door wider. She motions for me to come in and park my butt at the kitchen table. Her hands are on her hips. I'm in for a mother-daughter showdown.

I explain. "I don't have a clue how to act around challenged kids. I'm pretty challenged myself." I hope this gets me off the hook, but Mom isn't saying anything. "Um, what's a camp counselor get paid?"

"First of all," Mom says, "you aren't old enough to be a camp counselor. You would be a volunteer, and volunteers don't get paid. And second, your only challenge is that you are my beautiful daughter who has led a charmed life. You have lots to offer. You're funny; you're smart; you have a good heart; you are strong. Spread the love, Bernie. Spread some of you." Mom whirls her hands in the air, presses them to her chest, and then pushes the invisible love toward me.

"But, Mom—"

Mom squeezes my shoulder a little, and gives me the listen-to-your-mother look. There must be a manual that teaches moms how to shame their children into doing what they want. I get it. I don't have a choice. I'm Smile Academy's newest volunteer.

"Report to Miss Robyn at the academy at nine-thirty tomorrow morning. Craft time starts at ten. You can leave before or after lunch. In the afternoon, the kids go outside to play or the counselors take them for a walk around town."

"Whatever. Sure," I tell Mom, even though I'd rather spend my free time at the skate park.

The next morning, I fly out of bed with ollies, pop shove-its, heel flips, kick flips, and half-pipes on my mind. Then reality sinks in. I'm helping at Smile Academy. The highlight of my day will consist of keeping kids from eating glue sticks. And I won't be coming home with extra cash, which means no new skateboard in my future.

Smile Academy opened in the beginning of the summer, but I've never paid much attention to it. I pass the old Victorian house with the wrap-around porch and smiley-face daisy sign on the way to the skate park, but it's always been just another Main Street business. I make a mental note to avoid the huge crack by their driveway when I go by, but that's the most thought I've ever given the place.

Today, I don't pass it. I stop and slowly walk up the creaky wooden steps.

"Bernice! Wait! Let me catch up, please." Odelia is walking quickly toward me. Her tangerine gown makes a swishy sound. Her tiara is hanging by a few curls.

"What are you doing here?" I ask.

"I wanted to see you again," she says cheerfully, adjusting her tiara. "Where are *we* going?"

"*I'm* volunteering at Smile Academy, a camp for kids who were born with Down syndrome."

"I see. *We* are helping children in a social atmosphere. Good. That will give me a chance to watch you. I can see that you've combed your hair." Odelia sniffs the air around me, "And you smell like strawberries. Very nice!"

I ignore her compliment. "Do you even know what Down syndrome is?" I ask.

"No. I suppose these children live *down* around the bend, in the less fortunate side of town."

It's no surprise that Odelia is clueless about Down syndrome. "That's not what it is," I say. "But if you have to shadow me, let's get going. I'm already late."

I leave my skateboard on the porch, open the door, and duck inside. The walls are painted light blue with bright smiley-face daisies stenciled along the top. A long hallway shoots out in front with wide doors leading into separate rooms. Smile Academy may be a summer camp, but it looks a whole lot like a school.

The noise hits me next. Lots of laughing, singing, and friendly yelling, followed by more laughing, singing, and yelling. What have I gotten myself into?

"I prefer quiet, well-behaved children," Odelia whispers to me.

"I prefer stinky skateboarders."

We knock on a glass office door. A lady about thirty years old motions us to come in. She introduces herself as Miss Robyn. Miss Robyn is tall and thin and supermodel beautiful. She belongs on a runway, not in a place filled with noisy kids. She tells us she's confused because she was expecting one volunteer, not two. I introduce Odelia, and Miss Robyn says she's grateful for all the help she can get. I get the feeling she wants to ask Odelia why she's dressed like a princess, but she doesn't. Maybe she's afraid she'll scare her extra volunteer away.

Miss Robyn gives us fast and furious instructions about what we can and can't do with the kids. Mostly, I'm a gofer. I run for supplies for the counselors, and if they need help with something else, they'll call me. I'm not supposed to actually play with the kids or go outside with them, which I appreciate. No one from the skate park can know I hang out at Smile Academy.

Miss Robyn tells Odelia she is responsible for story time. She hands Odelia a thick book of fairy tales, and Odelia lights up like the fluorescent bulbs above her.

For the first hour, I'm a gofer, all right. A real gopher! Just like the furry creature who lives under our shed, I'm *buried* in the supply closet searching for blue paint, white paper, masking tape, and felt squares. And I don't like it one bit! The place smells like a mixture of stationery supplies, cleaning junk, and stale crackers. I could sure use some fresh air. When I'm finally asked to bring colored pencils to the playroom, I'm more than happy to.

As I divide the pencils among the tables, the kids' eyes follow me. I feel like I'm under a spotlight. And after Miss Robyn introduces me, they call out my name. "Bernice! Bernice!" Every time I leave and come back, it's the same. "Bernice! Bernice!" I want to shrink into my sneakers. In the back of my mind, I'm making up excuses to not volunteer here anymore.

Odelia's not having a great day either. She's stiff as a statue in the rocking chair. She's reading, but her voice is flat like she's going over a complicated recipe. The three kids on the floor in front of her are not interested in her story. One is lying down, humming. Another is collecting lint on the rug, and a third is thumbing through a picture book.

Odelia licks a finger, flips a page with an exaggerated toss of her wrist, and tries again and again to make them listen. When she finishes with, "And they lived happily ever after," no one moves or claps. Odelia slams the book shut and struts over. "These children are disrespectful. I don't want to read to them anymore."

"Get over yourself, princess," I tell her. "You are a lousy storyteller. Try being more entertaining."

Odelia barks, "These bad children should—"

"Stop, Odelia." I pull her over to the corner. "These are not bad children. They may be wired differently than me and you, and they may get on our nerves, but so what? Put on your best princess patience and get back to story hour."

I had to stick up for the kids. That, and it felt good to put Odelia in her place for once instead of the other way around.

Odelia hikes up her dress and retreats to her rocker. Five kids follow her, smiling brightly. She can't see it but she's their royal ruler. They're happy to follow her anywhere.

Miss Robyn pulls me aside. "Your friend, Odelia, she's not from around here?"

"She told me she used to live on an estate, in Europe, maybe?" I explain. "Out in the middle of nowhere."

"I see," Miss Robyn says quietly, "She's probably not had any interaction with many types of people, including special needs children. In that case, let the children be the teachers."

I'm confused. "The kids will help Odelia be more . . ."

"Accepting of differences," Miss Robyn adds. "Bernice, I've been meaning to tell you. There's a girl who has been begging me to have you sit with her. Can you do that for a while? Nellie wants to show you how she can write her name. I believe that her mom—your mom's friend, Barb O'Malley—told her you'd be coming. She's been very excited."

Nellie is a ten-year-old with enough energy to light a small city. Her paper is filled with letters written in capital letters at odd angles. I park myself down the bench from her, not wanting to disobey Miss Robyn's rule of personal space. That's a lie. I feel uncomfortable being close to Nellie. I want to keep my distance.

"You are Bernice!" Nellie hollers, even though I'm within four feet. Nellie's plump body jiggles as if an electrical current is running through it. The curls that frame her almond-shaped eyes and slightly flat nose jiggle, too.

Yes, I am Bernice. No kidding. Now even the camp hamster in the corner knows my name. Nellie keeps jiggling and calling "Bernice!" and her jiggling is catching. I find myself jiggling close enough to smell her shampoo. When I do, she suddenly takes my face in her hands. Her tongue peeks out from behind her lower lip. I can't tell if she's upset or happy.

"Bernice smells!" Nellie shouts.

Oh, no! Miss Robyn, where are you? Help!

Next, Nellie puts on a super-sized grin. "Bernice smells like fruit, like me. Bernice is my BFF! Nellie Frances O'Malley and Bernice are BFFs!"

This kid is a real charmer. A cutie-patootie, as Dad would say. I gently pull Nellie's fingers away. "Show me your stuff, BFF," I say, smiling.

Nellie's lips pucker as if she's bitten into a sour apple. I am an idiot. I speak softer and slower, and explain directions in a way that I think will be easier for Nellie to understand. "Show. Me. How. You. Make. Your. letters."

Nellie rolls her eyes. "Bernice talks funny," she says. "BFFs should be nice. Bernice should say *please*." The please comes out extra loud. Every kid in the playroom stops what they're doing. Odelia stops reading. The teachers pause. A dark-haired boy named Joe drops his paintbrush and gives me a thumbs-up sign.

I get it! I get it! "*Please* show me how you write your letters?"

Nellie marks the paper using the same concentration I muster up for English essays. It takes her a full fifteen minutes—I know; I've watched the clock—but at the end, Nellie Frances O'Malley is written neatly on a line in block letters. Her handwriting is better than mine.

"Bernice is proud of Nellie?" she asks.

It's a fact. I am proud, and I'll tell her so. "Nellie Frances O'Malley is made of awesome."

Nellie gives me the tightest hug I've ever gotten from somebody other than a relative. She chants, "Made of awesome! Made of awesome!" and doesn't let up until Miss Robyn lines up the campers to go outside, and the door to the playground shuts.

Odelia and I collapse into nearby bean bag chairs. Well, I collapse. Odelia tests it out, then folds herself into it like a crystal vase in bubble wrap.

"What a day," I say. "I'm beat."

Odelia's eyes widen. "You don't look as if you were beaten."

I don't know where to begin, so I shake my head and let it go.

Odelia wipes her brow with her tissue. "I've been beaten, also. On the inside. Every part of my patience has been challenged. You can bet your bloomers that I'll think twice about coming here again."

I am too tired for this conversation. At first, like Odelia, I felt overwhelmed—the smells, the noise, the kids, and I hated the thought of coming back. But now, I'm already looking forward to Thursday.

The Wicked Truth

On the way back to our block, Odelia gives me an earful about how terrible Smile Academy is, and I run defense. I tell her what I understand about Down syndrome, which isn't much. The only solid fact I have is that kids with Down syndrome are born with an extra chromosome. I remember this from third grade, when Lindsay Melsing moved to town and became part of our class. Before she showed up, my teacher made a big deal about how Lindsay was born with a birth defect and that we should accept her, be nice to her, and never make fun of her. When I met Lindsay, I noticed that her arms were kind of short, and when she walked, it seemed as if her upper body was in a hurry and the rest shuffled along trying to catch up. She was uncoordinated during gym class, but so was half the class. Lindsay wouldn't let anything bother her. If she had trouble, she'd shrug it off and tell a joke. By the end of the school year she had more friends than I did.

While I'm telling all of this to Odelia, she chews on her lip, taking it in.

"The campers like you," I say.

"They like me?" Odelia asks.

I nod and this encourages her. She bugs me with endless questions I can't answer. I tell her I'm not an expert, but she keeps going. Finally, I shout, "Down syndrome is not some awful disease. It's not their fault. Just like it's not your fault that your stupid godmother has all these requirements of you, but she lets you get away with anything."

"For example?" Odelia asks tersely.

"Like dressing up in ridiculous princess outfits. I don't care if you are a real princess; no one does that."

"But I've dressed like this, ever since—"

I cut her off. "Your godmother wants you to be happy. Looking like a character who belongs in a theme park makes you happy. Serena's taken the easy way out. She doesn't force you to be normal. So there." That should shut Odelia up.

Odelia's lips stay zipped. When we get to my house, she follows me inside. I've gotten so used to her being around, I almost forget that Mom and Dad have no idea who she is.

"Who do we have here?" Mom asks.

"This is Odelia. She volunteers at Smile Academy. She was the storytelling princess."

Odelia extends her hand, as if she's expecting Mom to kiss it. Mom shakes her hand, hard, and asks about our day. I tell her how I spread the love as she requested. Mom pats my cheek and reaches for her purse. "Back in a jiff," she calls. "You two have fun."

"Your mother is sweet," Odelia says. "I wish my mother and father were a part of my life. I was young when they passed. I don't remember much about them."

I'm not sure what to say. My life *is* pretty great, and Odelia's has been sad and . . . odd. Neither one of us says a word for a full minute. I turn on the faucet, fill a glass, and take a gulp of water.

"Remember the joke you made about me being Sleeping Beauty?" Odelia asks.

I nod and take a few more gulps.

"Sometimes I pretend that Sleeping Beauty *was* my mother."

"Why?"

"Serena tells me that my father caught my mother asleep in the woods one day. He thought she was beautiful and wanted to talk to her, so he woke her with a kiss. That was the beginning of their courtship."

"And they married, had you, and they died? The end?"

"Yes," Odelia says softly.

Another awkward silence sneaks into the room. I need to lighten things up. "No mean fairy who curses a baby? No wicked witch who casts a spell?"

Odelia runs her delicate fingers across the kitchen cabinets. "It's a short, sad tale."

"You've got me," I say, giving her a friendly punch in the arm.

"Bernice! Never, ever, *ever* use violence to get your point across. We'll talk about this in a later lesson." Odelia takes out her ODELIA'S GUIDE TO THE SOCIAL GRACES notebook and makes notes.

"No!" I say.

"Oh, yes! And in the meantime, don't hit me. I'm fragile."

I let a smirk escape in her direction before hopping up on the counter. "I'm starving. Let's get lunch. What do you want?"

Odelia pulls out a kitchen chair, sits, and folds a napkin on her lap. "I'd like a spinach and carrot stew with baby potatoes, please. And a large glass of freshly squeezed grapefruit juice."

I think it's funny that Odelia expects me to get this for her. "I hate to tell you this, Odelia, but we don't have a chef who whips up meals for us." I expect her to put up a fuss, but when she just looks down and closes her eyes for a second, my heart bends a bit.

In the fridge, I find two juice boxes and put one in front of Odelia. I walk to the pantry and grab the peanut butter, jelly, and bread. I get two butter knives from the drawer, use one to make my sandwich, and offer the other to Odelia.

Odelia studies the knife for a second. Then she lets out a weary sigh and makes her own sandwich.

When we're both done, I put our lunches in plastic wrap. "We're taking them to go," I say, and yank Odelia from her chair. "We're going to the skate park."

Odelia doesn't quite get the meaning of a sandwich to go. As we walk, she doesn't take a bite. Instead, she picks at the crust and leaves a trail that Hansel and Gretel would appreciate. Long habits—in this case, Odelia's habit of sitting properly at a table and being served—must be hard to break.

As soon as we get to the park, Odelia finds her spot on the bleachers. She places a napkin on her lap and dives in. I hurry for the gate, hoping that no one has noticed I showed up with a princess.

There's a sign posted:

ATTENTION SKATERS AGES 11–14!

COMPETE IN THE LAWRENCE COUNTY SKATE-OFF
SATURDAY, AUGUST 15TH AT NOON
PORCHTOWN SKATE PARK

Prizes awarded.
Entertainment by No Boys Allowed

A skate-off! And my favorite band's a part of it? Wow! I reach for an entry form stapled to the sign and read it quickly. I can do only four out of the five required tricks to qualify for the competition. "Fiddlesticks!"

"Dude, say *what*? You ready to rock this?"

I recognize that voice, and eye contact with its owner is out of the question. "Maybe," I spit out. I hide behind the entry form and feign intense interest in it. I hear Odelia inside my head: *Be a pine tree, never a willow.* And I stand slightly taller. More like a skinny shrub.

Wyatt says nothing. I say nothing. Here we go again. Fiddle, fiddle. Fiddle with the entry form. Fiddlesticks!

Wyatt takes my silence as his clue to leave. I can't blame him. He obviously can't talk to a person who isn't talking back.

"Later, Dude," Wyatt says, and I peek around the paper in time to see him sailing away on his board toward the half-pipe.

I'm a disgrace to the social graces. Why didn't I say something, *anything* to Wyatt about how much I wanted to be a part of the skate-off. He. Was. Right. There. I failed. He bailed.

After I spin around the park for a half hour, carefully avoiding Wyatt, I roll to the gate and flip my board into my hands. I motion for Odelia to follow me home, and I fill her in. "Wyatt wanted to talk to me, and I . . . I . . ."

"You said nothing?" Odelia asks.

"Almost nothing. What can I do?" I ask her. "What can I say to him when I see him?"

"I've been contemplating a lesson that may be helpful." Odelia takes out her notebook, and reads:

"ODELIA'S GUIDE TO THE SOCIAL GRACES

LESSON 4: GENUINE GREETINGS

OBJECTIVE: Bernice will learn to master conversational beginnings. Like a skilled weaver, she will use appropriate greetings to weave relationships with her elders and her peers. (Note to self: To Bernice, a greeting consists of mumbles and snorts, similar to those made by a snoring octogenarian.)"

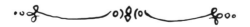

"What a mouthful! And I don't sound like a generic octopus."

Odelia pinches the bridge of her nose as if trying to ward off a big headache. "An *octogenarian* is someone who is eighty-plus years."

She may be a clueless princess, but there's a good amount of brainpower under that tiara. Her vocab would make a college professor proud. Still, I'm not entirely stupid. "I may not know what an octogenarian is, but I can carry on a conversation with *most* people."

"Bernice, you cannot hold a conversation with Wyatt or any boy, and you know it. When a boy asks a question, how do you answer?"

"Fine. Cool. Good. What up?" I would never say that last part, but I had to throw it out there.

"Those responses will get you nowhere. Try saying hello, and add his name. It shows you're glad to see him and you want to get to know him."

"No one says hello. Can I say hi?"

Odelia thinks about this as we walk the last block. Once we're in my living room, I expect a lecture, but she answers with a simple, "Yes."

"Then what?" I ask. "This is the part where I get stuck. It doesn't matter whether I'm trying to put Moron Forge—I mean, Ron Forge—in his place or whether it's someone like Wyatt who I want to impress. My brain turns to mush."

Odelia rubs her temples. "Ask how the person's doing or ask a simple question."

"That's your advice? That's it?" I hate that I'm pleading for help.

"I expect you to remember what we've covered in our past lessons. Be prepared to run into Wyatt. Always make sure you're squeaky clean and positively poised, be a pine tree, never a willow, and—"

"And what about the fact that I'm scared I'll faint in front of him?"

"You've got to be strong, Bernice! You want him to see you as friendly, don't you? You want to show him you're interested in what he says, don't you?"

"Yes!"

"And there's one more thing: maintain eye contact."

"You've got to be kidding! It's not that easy. It's like looking at a president. You want to, and you'll be sorry if you don't, but you can't. You just can't. It's too hard."

"We'll practice," Odelia says. "Pretend you're meeting me for the first time, and I am the most handsome prince in the land." Odelia coughs. "I mean the cutest boy in town."

"Can I pretend you're somebody else?" I ask. "Can you be Wyatt?"

Odelia nods. "Excellent suggestion." She struts over to the lime-green chair in the corner and sits, back straighter than straight, legs crossed, chin held high. "Hello, Bernice. I am Wyatt."

I shake my head. "Lose the posture, princess. And news flash! Wyatt doesn't know my name."

"Oh, I remember what he calls you. Let's try again." Odelia pulls the bobby pins out of her bun. Her hair falls to her shoulders and the tips of her ears peek out. She sinks down into the chair, kicks off her slippers, tucks a foot under her jumper, then bolts upright. "Oh, fiddlesticks! My jumper will get wrinkled! Serena despises wrinkles. She'll disapprove. I'll get into trouble!"

I run upstairs and pull out a pair of jeans and a maroon shirt that has the Porchtown Piranhas logo on it. It's my Field Day shirt from the spring, and there's no way I'm wearing anything that screams sixth grade in middle school. Back downstairs, I throw them at Odelia. "Change into this." Without a word, she goes into the bathroom and comes back as a regular kid. The tiara is still glued on, but I can ignore it.

Odelia sits in the chair again and lets her neck relax and her shoulders droop. She can slump? Odelia surprises me more and more every day.

"Hi, Wyatt," I say, holding back the giggles. "How are you?"

In a very fake, very low voice, Odelia answers, "I'm fine. I haven't seen you in a while. Where have you been, Dud?"

I laugh hard and long, but eventually spit out, "It's Dude! Not Dud."

"Oh. Dude," Odelia says, testing the word on her lips. She tries it out a second time using her Wyatt voice. "Duuude." This sends us both into hysterics. I swear I even hear Odelia snort.

We calm down enough to move on. "Where have you been, Dude?" Odelia asks. Before I can answer, she goes back into high-pitched princess mode, and asks, "Why in heaven's name does the boy call you that?"

I shrug. I have no idea. I answer Odelia's first question. "At home."

Odelia clears her throat. "Answer with complete thoughts in complete sentences."

"I. Have. Been. At. Home…"

Another dramatic throat-clearing from the princess.

"I am volunteering at a camp on Tuesday and Thursday mornings. Otherwise, I would gladly have exported myself to the park to partake in physical activity and perhaps a conversation or two with you." I add a snicker because . . . well, that sentence, complete with good vocabulary, deserves a snicker.

"You sound so grown up, Bernice!"

"I don't want to sound like a grown-up. I don't want to be a dork."

Odelia tilts her head. "I don't want you to be a duck either, Bernice."

"Not duck! Dork! Someone more socially awkward than my awkward self."

Odelia thinks about this for a minute, and then starts babbling about a new lesson. "During lesson five we'll delve into the art of crafty conversation," she says enthusiastically. "We'll talk about keeping conversations moving along. It'll be just ducky."

I shake my head like I'm thoroughly disgusted, but I feel the corners of my mouth turning up. "Odelia, I can't deal with any more conversation today. Maybe I'll just become a mime."

Odelia ignores my comment and makes some notes. I slide into a daydream where Wyatt and I are leaning against our lockers at Porchtown Middle, trading secrets like old friends. After a few minutes, I notice that Odelia has put down her pen and is gazing out our bay window. She hasn't hurried back to Miss Princess Posture Perfect yet. She's curled up in the chair; her tiara is dangling dangerously to the left, and she's doing some daydreaming of her own.

"Hey, you all right?" I ask.

"Mmm hmm," she answers.

"Answer with complete thoughts in complete sentences," I remind her.

Odelia touches the tip of her nose. "I'm fine, Bernice . . . but . . . you know . . . I haven't been completely honest with you. I haven't always been the well-behaved girl you see before you." She rubs her nostrils and if I didn't know better, I'd say she was tempted to pick what's hiding in there.

I wonder if it's full confession time—time that Odelia fesses up she's not royalty, and that her princess obsession has been nothing but a sneaky attempt to get attention.

Odelia explains, "Serena says my mother called me her little princess every day. But I didn't always act in a proper manner. I was horrid. I'd fight tooth and nail when it came time to put on fancy clothes. I hated dressing up. But at my mother's funeral, I finally put on the gown she loved to see me wear, a beautiful dress fit for her little princess. And ever since, I've taken it upon myself to be the perfect princess she wanted me to be."

This is not a joke. If my parents were gone, I'd probably dress like a vampire and only come out at night. Odelia hasn't had it easy, that's for sure. First her mom dies, then her dad. Could Odelia be using her princess ways to cope with the sadder than sad deal she got in life? Or . . . and I'll have to give this some serious thought: Odelia *really is* a princess and, just like the rest of us, she's trying desperately to fit in.

Odelia pulls herself out of the chair. "I need to change back into my gown. I'll feel better. Serena has high expectations, and she'll misunderstand if I'm not dressed as I usually am."

I want to tell Odelia that everything will turn out okay. I want to remind her that *I* have expectations, too. With her help, I expect to be less awkward by the end of this summer. I want to tell Odelia all of this, but she's scurrying out the door with barely a good-bye.

There Once Was a Caveman

I stay up the whole night worrying—about boys, about Odelia, about the skate-off. I *have* to be part of that competition. It will prove to Wyatt that I, Bernice Baransky, am cool, mature, and worthy of conversation. Wait. A. Minute. I'm starting to sound like Odelia!

As soon as I'm dressed, I hit the skate park. I go straight to the gate and reread the competition entry form.

I've practiced most of the tricks they expect to see, but I'm not one hundred percent sure I can pull them off without tripping. And I've got nothing for the half-pipe. N-O-T-H-I-N-G. Nothing.

I hear a roll and a screech near me, and move the paper enough to see it's Wyatt. He steps off his board and leans against the gate. I can't look at him because I'm thinking about my sweat—sweat that a second ago was nowhere, but that's now dripping from my sports bra to my waist.

"You up for this, Dude?" Wyatt asks.

"Um, I, uh . . ." I *do* sound like a snoring octogenarian! I take a deep breath. In and out and try again. "Yes. I guess." There. I made my best attempt.

I hear Odelia in the back of my brain. *Ask a simple question.* "Are you entering?"

Wyatt takes the form from me. It takes every smidgen of courage in my soul to look at him. He answers. "Yeah, Dude. It'll be off the wall."

And I've got zip. Nada. Nothing. My lips are stuck.

Wyatt steps back on his board and is about to take off. I catch sight of a tree swaying in the breeze, and it reminds me of what I should do. I pull myself up straighter, lock my eyes on his, and say, "Wait! I stink." I mentally slap myself upside my head. I'm as poised and intelligent as dirt. I try again. "I mean; I stink at kick flips."

"How's your ollie?" Wyatt wants to know.

"Decent," I answer. I hold my palms about a foot and a half off the ground to show him how high I can pop up my board. He didn't see my fingers shaking, right?

"We can work with that. The higher you pop your ollie, the better."

"They want a trick on the half," I blurt out.

"With a competition like this, it might not be so much about the tricks. It's probably about putting on a good show. You want me to help you?"

He wants to help me! I should shout for joy and thank him, but all I can do is nod. So I nod, twice.

"C'mon, Dude, time's a wastin'. Let's bounce."

I bounce. I bounce after Wyatt like a bunny rabbit.

Wyatt spends an entire hour with me. First, he teaches me foot placement for kick flips, and he touches my foot to help me get in the right position on my board. I don't faint, which is a big surprise, but I've gnawed off every fingernail except one. It's not such a big surprise that I can't keep the conversation going.

"Drag your front foot forward more!" he shouts as I ollie. "Kick toward the heel side of the nose. Like this."

I do what he shows me. I succeed in getting the board to rotate, but I can't land the trick. The board slides away, and I have nothing to step on but cement. My lack of talent is obvious. Wyatt suggests we move to the half-pipe to speed things up. Downhill, spine-tingling speed. Dang.

I'm relieved when Wyatt has me try a caveman on the half-pipe. This involves running only part of the way up and then jumping on the board and heading back down from there. I get up enough guts to do this a third of the way, then two-thirds. But I can't start from the top. The last time I tried that, the person I most wanted to impress had to check to see if I was alive.

"Don't worry, Dude. You'll get braver," Wyatt says as he leaves.

I'm extremely grateful he doesn't turn around because my cheeks match the red graphic on his skateboard deck. I holler, "Later!" and ride away wondering if Wyatt has a clue about my real name. Or if it even matters.

I find myself thinking about my morning and about Odelia. Part of me wants to brag about how I actually got up the nerve to say a few words to Wyatt. Part of me knows it was a lame attempt at intelligent conversation. I wouldn't mind Odelia's company. There's no one else who totally gets my Wyatt obsession.

After lunch, my cell rings. It's Roxanne. "Winnie's. Ten minutes. Be there."

I don't know how I'm going to keep it from Roxanne that the boy she hopes to see is one I've already seen today.

At Winnie's, Roxanne and I sit on top of a picnic table cooling off with our favorite icy treats. I ask her how things went in New York.

"Dumb and dumber," Roxanne answers. "The producer liked me for that acne commercial and my mom went insane with joy. Filming starts in a couple of weeks. With my luck, it'll air at the beginning of school. I'll be nicknamed Zit Girl or Dip Zit. Ugh." Roxanne looks around. "Do you think he'll come?"

"Who?" I ask, faking cluelessness.

"The one in the baseball uniform? Remember?"

And in that instant, the van pulls up and Wyatt steps out. He shouts, "Hey, Dude, awesome skate sesh." He salutes me with his glove and steps in line with his team.

Roxanne sidles up to me turning a sickly green. She hisses, "He knows who you are? I've been gone, what, like a couple of days!"

"His name is Wyatt. He skates," I explain.

"At that park? The park you hang out at?"

I nod. "He's helping me with the Lawrence County Skate-Off."

Roxanne doesn't ask about the skate-off. She's got boy on her brain. "So, it's not like he's your boyfriend?"

"NO! Not like that at all." I'm about to give her a nice *girlfriend* punch, but I remember Odelia's never-ever-*ever*-use-violence speech, and leave my fist anchored to my side. "I'm not even sure we're *friends*. He doesn't even know my name."

"Can I be his friend?" Roxanne asks. She slurps her treat and peeks out over the top of the big cup.

I shrug and act like I don't care. Roxanne and I don't say much to each other as we walk back to my house.

"Hey, Roxy, Super Stylist to the Stars, you want to come in and do my hair?" I ask.

Roxanne jumps and claps like a cheerleader. "Duh. YES!"

It doesn't take much to get me back on Roxanne's good side. She gabs about the latest hairstyles all the way to my room. She makes me stand in the middle and does a complete 360, walking around me, checking out my hair. She shoves it up, pats it down, and runs her fingers through the curls. "Did you always wear your bangs this way? To the side?" she asks.

I want to tell her it was Odelia's idea, but if I mention her, I'll have to update Roxanne on everything. I shrug a shoulder like I don't remember.

Roxanne studies my hair some more. "If you straighten those bangs, they won't sit like curly fries above your eyebrows."

I picture a poodle whose groomer brushes her matted fur until it's manageable. I'm about to be poodle-ized.

"Do you even own a straightener?" Roxanne asks.

"My mom bought me one for Christmas, but I haven't taken it out of the box. It's in the bathroom cabinet. Under the sink."

Roxanne squeals, "Christmas in July! While I'm getting that, you can hunt down a pair of sharp scissors."

The Big Bad Bug

Having dinner with Dad is like sitting in a room with air freshener called Dead Fish. He's been out since dawn scooping up defenseless minnows and clams to sell as bait in the store. "Six more weeks till school starts, Bern," he says through a mouthful of roast beef. "Middle school. Cool beans, kiddo." Dad gets up to put his plate in the sink and gives Mom a squeeze. "Great dinner, hon." He skips the minute-long thank-you-for-being-a-great-cook smooch, which I appreciate. "Ellie, our daughter is growing up," he reminds her.

"She's still my baby," Mom says, pinching my cheek. She gently moves her hand under my chin and tilts it toward the light. "There's a difference in you, but I can't decide what it is. Do you see it, George? Our daughter seems to have a spiffy new maturity about her."

"Right on," Dad adds.

Will my parents ever officially graduate to the current decade?

I pull away from Mom, tear off a piece of bread, eat it, and let lose a wet burp to convince them I'm not *that* mature. It amazes me that they can't figure out that Roxanne cut my hair three inches shorter, layered it, and straightened it.

"Odelia stopped by while you were out," Mom says. "She must have been coming from Smile Academy because she was dressed in the most funkadelic chartreuse gown I've ever seen. She said she'd stop back after dinner."

"Okay," I say. I've *got* to get Odelia out of those ridiculous gowns.

After I help Mom clean up the kitchen, I go across the street and knock on Odelia's door. A butler answers—a real, walking, breathing, dressed-like-a-penguin, butler! He introduces himself as Gerard, invites me in, and calls out, "Miss Odelia, a guest awaits you in the parlor."

I don't have to wait long for Odelia and that's a relief. She flies down a winding staircase, and says, "I was hoping you'd stop over. Let's go outside and talk."

I wasn't planning a full-out stroll with the princess. What if someone sees me?

After half a block of speed walking, Odelia slows down. "Bernice! Your hair! It's lost its curl. This often happens at puberty."

I am not discussing the P word with Odelia. No way. As Odelia attempts to fluff my bangs, I run defense. "My friend, Roxanne, cut it. And it got straight *on purpose* with this heated thing called a straightener. Short, straight hair is easy to take care of. I bet you think it's not right for me, but I like it, and—"

Odelia puts her hand on my shoulder. "Don't fret. I was about to say that it suits you. Now, tell me about Wyatt."

I fill Odelia in on what happened at the park.

"You talked to him. You didn't mumble? That's wonderful!" She darts around, and with that greenish yellow gown on, she reminds me of a big lightning bug. Before she gets out of control, she checks herself and smoothes out the wing-like ruffles that hang from her waist. No way could I ever rock a lightning bug dress like that. I'd look like a skinny glow worm.

A car full of kids cruises down our street, and I panic. I can't be seen walking next to Odelia! I imagine what they'd call us at Porchtown Middle: Beauty and Bernice or maybe Buggy Beauty and Beastly Bernice. Doesn't matter what. It'd all be bad. To play it safe, I duck behind a row of hedges.

Odelia keeps gliding down the sidewalk, yakking about social graces. She hasn't noticed my side trip. When I catch up to her, I hear her going on and on about how Wyatt shares the same good looks as Prince Chancellor Pomegranate. She's convinced that Chance (my name for him, not hers) and Wyatt would be fast friends. She sounds like any other boy-crazy thirteen-year-old.

"Have you ever actually spent any time with Chance . . . *Chancellor?*" I ask.

Odelia's caught off guard. "No. I've never had the chance." Odelia chuckles at her own joke. I chuckle, too. Truth is, her pun was pretty clever.

"Anyway," Odelia continues, "it'd be easy to speak to him. I once prepared a two-hour soliloquy on the life of a hummingbird. No one heard it, of course."

"You talked to yourself for two whole hours? Really, Odelia?"

"I can speak on any subject, to anyone, and that's why you need me.

But you'll need to get over being embarrassed to be seen with me." Odelia hikes up her "wings" and flits away.

I wish Odelia hadn't caught me hedge-hopping. I feel bad. I call out to her, "If the next time we're out in public, you promise to not wear the princess gear, I'll do the next lesson. C'mon, Odelia, I do need you and your lessons. I can't figure out how to keep talking to Wyatt. It's hard. Especially when I'm concentrating on skateboarding tricks. Can you help me?"

Odelia spins around. "Yes, I'll help, and if it'll make you happy, I'll put on regular, boring clothes." She whips out the pink notebook, and says:

"ODELIA'S GUIDE TO THE SOCIAL GRACES

LESSON 5: THE ART OF CRAFTY CONVERSATION

OBJECTIVE: Bernice will learn how to fine-tune the conversational skills she's acquired so far. Just like a vocalist whose simple notes build to an elaborate musical crescendo, Bernice will sing her heart out to capture the attention of her prince.(Note to self: I've heard Bernice sing, and I'm grateful that the singing I speak of here is metaphorical.)"

Odelia grins at me like she's got the key to my life. Then she belts out a musical scale that would make an opera star proud.

"This is crazy," I say. "I am not a singer."

"Oh, I know," Odelia says. "My objective is to have you engage in an ongoing conversation, and then Wyatt will get to know you better. He'll see the real you."

Odelia needs to follow her own advice because I haven't seen the real Odelia yet—the one who used to hate dresses and hate being proper. I want to meet *that* Odelia.

I find a bus stop bench on a side street; we both sit down, and Odelia continues. "A conversation is like a game of chess," she instructs. "You take a turn. Wyatt takes a turn. If you don't move the pieces on the board, you don't give him a chance to join in, and the game ends." Odelia sings again as she moves imaginary chess pieces across the bench's wooden planks.

I put my face in my hands, and mumble, "Can we stop with the singing and the games?" I peek out between my fingers to make sure no one has stopped to see Odelia's show.

"It sounds as if you did well with Wyatt on your last visit to the park.

But you must *keep* asking questions—questions that will get Wyatt to talk for a longer period of time. Make sure you ask questions where you'll get more than a yes or no answer."

"I thought I did that when I told him I can't pull off the tougher tricks."

"Choose your words carefully, Bernice. Do not make the conversation—"

I butt in before Odelia finishes. "I can't do this. I just can't. It's too much. Sure, I want Wyatt's attention, but I can't beg for it. Roxanne and the more popular girls know how to get *anybody's* attention, easily. I don't. I only dream about being the popular girl. Like the other night. I dreamt that everybody wanted to be me. Everybody gushed over me. And copied me. Even in my dream it was way too much to take. I woke up in a cold sweat."

Odelia flies off the bench. "First, never interrupt a speaker! It's rude. Second, no one wants to be part of a conversation that's one-sided, like the conversation you just had with yourself! Chess game, remember? Back and forth, back and forth. Ask about the other person—their hopes, their dreams. Don't overpower friends with *your* dreams. Don't sing out selfish speeches. Don't go into detail about you, you, YOU!"

Hello, big bad Odelia. Nice to meet you!

"Okay, Okay! I get it," I say, calming down. "But what if I need to tell someone off, or what if someone is boring me?"

"Speak the song of your heart," Odelia says.

Like I'm supposed to know what that means.

"What I mean is, speak your mind. Be kind. Be truthful. If someone or something is bothering you or boring you, turn the conversation around, or be polite and make your escape."

Lesson five is not for wimps! I get up and stretch and tell Odelia I will try. Then I add, "Right now, I need to get home. It's getting dark, and my mom's probably worried."

Odelia pouts. "I was enjoying our banter."

I smile at my clueless princess. "I'm making my escape, Odelia. Maybe we can banter tomorrow."

I leave Odelia sitting on the bench. If I were smarter and quicker, I could've put the Art of Crafty Conversation lesson to good use and gotten Odelia to talk about herself. Maybe if she opens up, she'll change into a normal human being.

The street light comes on and it shines on the neighborhood princess. Again, she reminds me of a lightning bug, a lonely lightning bug. But that bug better fly home soon before a policeman throws a net over her and carries her away.

The Wimpy Dragon Slayer

The wind is stronger than usual today. I hope it's not a nor'easter brewing because three days of bad weather will totally mess up my practice schedule. With any luck, it'll die down by the time I'm done at Smile Academy. If I'm found moping around the house, Mom will include me in her conversation with her supplies. Not that I couldn't use the practice.

Odelia isn't at the academy today. I have no idea why. I picture her walking aimlessly around her mansion trying to figure out how to impress Serena. What would it take to impress that godmother?

A camper named Timothy is busy *not* impressing Miss Robyn. He's hopscotching across the playroom using the squares on the linoleum. With Miss Robyn's permission, I do my best to hopscotch him back to his seat. He sits there until I turn around, then he's at it again. Angelo thinks this is hysterical, and joins in Timothy's game. Angelo laughs like a hyperactive hyena and it's contagious. Soon every kid is hopscotching and giggling. Miss Robyn stops the chaos and puts on a movie about taking care of pets. In one scene, a dog pees on a newspaper and makes a funny design. The highlight of my day comes when shy Sammy asks if he can try that.

By one o'clock, the wind's turned into a bearable breeze, and I'm at the park. Wyatt is nowhere, and this day has a friendless vibe about it. With the exception of an old fart who's reliving his youth, and two shortie shredders, I have every obstacle to myself, including the half-pipe. I warm up by practicing the tricks I have to do for the skate-off: ollies, pop shove-its, and grinds. I have to be able to nail the easier 50-50 grind, which shouldn't be a problem. If I want to score points, I should pull off a complete 5-0 grind. Not going to happen.

When I take a water break, I see Odelia perched on the bleachers. I check her out twice because she's minus one princess gown and one princess tiara. She has on a baggy tunic-type thing in an obnoxiously bright coral color fit for a Florida grandmom. It's better than the jumper she wore to Winnie's. Not as lacy. No less geeky. She's resting her chin on a palm and has bored written all over her milky complexion.

"Hey," I call. "Why didn't you come to camp this morning?"

Odelia answers, "I had an appointment with a nosy doctor who wanted nothing more than for me to relate my life's story. And now I'm in a foul mood."

I wonder if Odelia's doctor is a therapist who is helping her get her head on straight. I can tell she doesn't want to fill me in, so I change the subject by asking, "You want to skate?"

Odelia pounces off the bleacher seat, and shouts, "Yes, Bernice! I would! Can you teach me?"

In half a minute, she's by my side. I can't resist this—what was that word she used? Serendipitous. I can't resist this serendipitous turn of events. In my most stuffy voice, I tell Odelia, "I will now proceed to teach you how to skateboard." I take out an invisible notebook, and read:

"BERNICE'S GUIDE TO SOCIAL SKATEBOARDING

LESSON 1: STANCE

OBJECTIVE: Odelia will learn where to place her slippered feet so that after she pushes off, she will balance deliberately on the skateboard and will not land on her strong gluteus maximus. (Odelia has the feet of a giant. Like size ten, at least. And the butt of an Olympic gymnast.)"

Odelia checks out her feet, tilting them left and right. She tries to check out her butt, but ends up wiggling like a dog chasing her tail.

"I'm enormous?" she asks.

I put my hand on her shoulder. "No. No way. I was only messing with you. I meant—"

She takes my hand and holds it. "You speak the truth."

"Just say okay," I tell her.

Odelia nods. "Oh . . . Kay. Serena insists I look like a brick house, meaning that I'm stiff and strong. I've never figured out if being compared to a house is good or bad. Can you teach a brick house how to skate?"

"If you're a brick house, then I'm the skinny mortar. We'll stick together." I pick up each one of Odelia's feet and put them on a specific spot on my skateboard. Then I peel away the fingernails that are digging into my shoulders, and give her a teeny shove. "Go!" I yell. "Bend your knees!"

Odelia's body tips and her arms flail about like they're not attached, but she stays on. Her balance is incredible! After fifteen minutes, she's pushing off on her own and yelling, "Wah hoo!" like every other newbie who scores a ride.

I rest against the chain link fence and think about my day. I can't remember the last time I had this much fun. Roxanne and I don't have this much fun anymore. With Roxanne, it's all about *her*. When's her next audition? What's her mom forcing her to do now? What's the latest hairstyle? Who is the cutest boy she knows? Roxanne could benefit from lesson five on conversation. She's not interested in what I do, and she never asks about my life, except if something's in it for her. Like the fact that she wants me to call her before I hit the park, so she can show up and I can introduce her to Wyatt. I just remembered I forgot to do this.

Soon Odelia catches up to me. "I'm finished with this unforgiving slab," she says, shoving my skateboard into my arms.

Her cheeks are flushed and her eyebrows are wet with sweat, yet she's smiling. When she takes off my helmet, she shakes her tangled hair, but doesn't attempt to fix it. "However," Odelia continues. "I'm asking Roderick, our carpenter, if he can make me a skateboard. Skateboarding is exhilarating! Of course, Serena won't approve." Odelia's eyes twinkle like a two-year-old with a secret.

"You're a natural," I tell her. "Next time, I'll show you some easy tricks."

With that, I ride into the park to rip up and down the volcano. The half-pipe stands a short distance away, snarling at me, mocking me. It's a surly, ugly dragon that'll attack me if I don't attack it first. I may be crazy, but I have to go for it.

I start from my comfort zone—the middle. After a few runs where, shock of all shockers, I don't do a faceplant into the vert, I get up the nerve to crawl closer and closer to the top before dropping in. But the higher I go, the more afraid I become. When fear shuts down my lungs, I stomp off the pipe. I wonder if Wyatt has a trick for the Lawrence County Skate-Off that's suitable for a wuss like me.

Cheers come from the bleachers. "Go, Bernice! Way to go, Bernice!" It's the kids from Smile Academy! They're sitting with Miss Robyn.

I skate over to find out why they're here.

"Field trip," Miss Robyn explains. "Our first time to the park. We never expected you to be here. Nellie is beyond excited that her new BFF is a star skateboarder." Miss Robyn shoots a glance to Nellie, and Nellie uses this opportunity to charge at me and bowl me over with a crushing hug.

Robbie and Claire, two other camp kids, join in. Soon all eight munchkins want hug time, and I'm surrounded. When the kids spot Odelia, a new hug-a-thon begins. Like me, Odelia is overwhelmed. At first, we don't hug back, but it's impossible to resist a bunch of cheery huggers.

"Don't let us interrupt your skating," Miss Robyn says. "I hope the kids aren't bothering you. We can go if we're causing too much of a commotion."

It's both nice and completely uncomfortable to have the Smile Academy kids as my personal cheerleaders. The hardcore skaters might think it's not cool, but the park is still pretty empty. So, for now, I want them to hang around. "Don't go," I tell her.

"Odelia," Miss Robyn calls, "care to sit with us?"

Before Odelia can answer, Angelo and Joe take Odelia's hands and pull her to the bleachers. Both boys fight to see who gets to sit on her lap. In the end, Odelia gives up and balances a nine-year-old on each knee, and is smooshed under their weight. I can't tell if she's upset or not. She's hidden behind bobs of black and brown hair.

I cruise away and roll up and down the mini-ramp, getting enough air to do a tail grab. Nothing special. But from the cheers you would've thought I did a varial flip—rotating my board from nose to tail, flipping it from top to bottom. Sort of like a combo of a pop shove-it and a kick flip. I haven't mastered that stupid kick flip, so a varial is totally out of my league.

Next, because I'm feeling cocky, I flip my board into my hands and walk over to the half-pipe. I do the caveman crawl. To. The. Top.

Before I overthink it and chicken out, I jump on, and drop in. I'm a warrior in battle against this dragon. My balance rocks as I find my sweet spot on the vert and sail across the bottom. The whole time I'm thinking: *I did it. I dropped in!* But what I didn't think about was what would happen next. I start to fly up the other side of the U, but there's no way I can pull off a turn and get back down in one piece. Halfway up I stop, drop, and roll like Fireman Fred taught us in first grade. I was so close!

I leave the half-pipe and practice my other tricks. For a half-hour straight, my cheerleaders go ballistic any time I do anything. They make me feel like a superstar.

When Miss Robyn leads the campers to the gate, I skate over quickly and give each kid a subtle, low high-five. "See you tomorrow, mighty munchkins. You are made of awesome."

They leave shouting, "Made of awesome! Made of awesome! Mighty munchkins are made of awesome!"

So much for subtle.

I head for the low rail in the back corner of the park, and suddenly catch an earful of laughter. I pick out one boy's laugh, and my skin turns to ice. Wyatt. He's outside the fence on the pool side. He must've seen me talking to the Smile Academy kids, and thinks it's hysterical. Oh, no!

There's a lump in my throat the size of a cantaloupe. I skate to the far side of the park, and when I look over my shoulder I see Wyatt pulling his friends away.

All the crafty conversation in the world won't fix this.

Once Upon a Style

Roxanne is on another Big Apple trip. She texted me to complain about it. Mother Nature decided to hike up the temperature and the newscasters make it sound like it's the end of the world: "Ninety-two degrees with a real-feel temperature of one-hundred-five. Heat advisory. Drink plenty of water. Stay indoors. Dangerous ozone levels. Safe sun time is ten minutes." We live in Pennsylvania, not on Mars. It's hot. Get over it. It's summer.

Mom insists I'll get heat exhaustion at the skate park, so she's forcing me to stay home. She has no idea how much I love her for that. I can't show my face there. What if Wyatt's found out that I not only talk to the campers from Smile Academy, but I volunteer there? No way will he want to hang with me. No way will he keep helping me with skate tricks.

Mom finds inside chores for me like laundry, dusting, and sock matching. I feel like I'm back in preschool. "Match items with like items," Miss Karen used to tell us. Mom hopes the cleaning and organizing will mask the sweaty smell of my skateboarding gear. Not going to happen. That's the smell of smacking, cracking, pounding, and rolling, and I'm not ditching it in favor of lemon furniture polish.

I try on old clothes to see what I need to get through the summer. On a scale of one to ten with ten being the most exciting thing in the world, this is a minus five. After a quick overview of what fits, I have to admit that I can use a few shirts. And something more than the sports bra Mom calls my training bra. *Boobilage.* Dang.

I'm standing in my room in my underwear, and Odelia walks in. I grab a tee and shorts and throw them on. "Mom let you in?"

"Yes, and we had a perfect conversation," she answers.

I shake my head because . . . well, that comment deserves a good head shake. I take in the whole Odelia scene. She has on a horseback riding outfit, complete with riding boots and weird leather things attached to her legs. I have no idea whether she's wearing a regular riding outfit or something from the Dark Ages.

"Stop staring at me, Bernice," Odelia pleads. She blushes, smoothes out her jacket, and attempts to flatten her puffed-out pants. "I had a riding lesson today with my trainer and my horse, Magnifico. We rode to the store. I made a purchase."

I picture Odelia riding up to the local Stop 'n Go, and parking her horse. I stifle a giggle. "Show me what you bought."

Odelia opens a leather bag, pulls out five teen magazines, and spreads them on my bed. Every celebrity from current hip-hop stars to who's hot in TV look up at me. I don't know what to think.

"Look at this girl. She's barely clothed!"

"It's a bikini," I tell her. "A bathing suit."

"I see," Odelia says. "I thought these pictures might help me help you with your style, but . . . oh, well." Odelia perks up. "I still have an idea for you:

ODELIA'S GUIDE TO THE SOCIAL GRACES

LESSON 6: DRESS TO IMPRESS

OBJECTIVE: Bernice will acquire an individual style that incorporates fashionable trends. (Note to self: Bernice's style to date resembles that of Lucan, a young boy from my former town who wears nothing but ill-fitting pants and dirty shirts. Lucan's sole purpose in life is to hop on rocks in the stream, pretending it's a moat filled with angry alligators.)"

Lucan is obviously a pretty cool kid. "Did you ever hop across that stream?" I ask.

"No. I do morning stretches, afternoon strolls, and have structured horseback riding lessons. And most recently, skateboarding." Odelia's eyes brighten when she says skateboarding, like skating is magical or something.

"That's it? Haven't you ever gone all out, gotten so wild that sweat drips off your eyelashes?"

"To perspire is not ladylike," Odelia answers slowly. "That's what Serena says."

I get the distinct feeling she's not buying what she's selling. She pulls me in close.

"In the late evening, I go out to an open field beyond our home, and—" She cuts off mid-sentence, covers her mouth, and whispers, "And I run. I run like a wild deer. I like running as much as skateboarding. But Serena doesn't approve of anything sporty, so I have to be careful."

"Don't you get tired of Serena's rules?" I ask. Before she can answer, I grab Odelia's hand and don't let go until we're outside. Then I take off down the driveway, and yell, "Bet you can't catch me!"

Odelia checks across the street to make sure Serena's not peering out of a window. Then she chases me to the end of the block and back. And wow! Is she fast! It's as if a weight's been lifted off her shoulders.

Exhausted, we fall on the lawn. Dad mowed the grass yesterday and the fresh, earthy smell tickles our noses. It reminds me of when I was little, and I'd set up a princess picnic out here on the grass and invite my stuffed animal servants.

I decide to roll down the hill, and Odelia does the same. We giggle like a bunch of preschoolers. At the bottom, we sit up and pick off the loose grass pieces that have stuck to our clothes.

"Fiddlesticks!" Odelia shouts, attempting to wipe away the green stains. "I've ruined my riding outfit. I'll have to hide these clothes until new ones can be made by Serena's favorite seamstress."

"You don't need a seamstress. My mom can wash these. And you can borrow a shirt and shorts from me."

Odelia claps her hands. "I'd be so grateful."

"Cool," I say.

"Cool," Odelia mimics. She does an enormous inhale like a yoga instructor. "I like the outdoors. Serena keeps me cooped up too much."

Back in my room, Odelia changes while I plug my phone into my speakers and crank up a playlist.

"I've never heard such loud music," Odelia comments. She flops on my bed and clicks her heels to the beat of a bass guitar.

Together we leaf through the magazines. Odelia stops on an article about an eighteen-year-old who is on safari. "My life is planned for me." Her voice is scratchy and sad. "Given different circumstances, I'd venture away from Serena's strict rule and expand my horizons. I'd travel the world and live in strange cultures, like the one pictured here. It's Africa. I'd love to see Africa! I'd run up and down hills, ride elephants, and chase cheetas in automobiles called Jeeps."

Whoa! Odelia dreams of more than proper behavior and princes? I show her a picture of a girl standing near a volcano, wearing hiking gear and carrying a camera. She takes a minute to study it, then flips it shut.

"We have much to do today. Serena is happy we've become friends. She says our shared experiences have enlightened us both. I won't spoil her opinion. Let's continue with our lesson on style. I've seen a portion of your clothing, but where might I find the rest of your wardrobe?" She sits up and waits for me to show her the secret room where my clothes are hiding.

I tell Odelia that what she's seen is it, and this makes her shudder like she's caught a random chill. We sit on the bed and find some normal-looking clothes in the teen magazines. We cut out pictures of tees, shirts, shorts, skirts, boots, and shoes. Odelia puts in her two cents about outfits in specific colors that are supposedly perfect for my body type and coloring. With my blonde hair, I should be wearing warm colors like orange, yellow, and peach, she tells me. No gray. No black. She's got to be kidding! A skateboarder minus the black is like Santa minus his red. Odelia does have a good eye, though. She shows me clothes that aren't exactly girly, but girly with an edge.

"Style should reflect your personality," she says. "You have the heart of an adventurer."

"I don't do adventure. That's *your* dream."

"Bernice, the next time you are at the skate park, take note of how many girls are there. I have seen none. You are fearless and strong, and when not skateboarding, you can portray your adventuresome spirit with the right clothes."

Maybe a fashion makeover *is* a good idea. Middle school kids rock a certain style, and it's not skater grunge, that's for sure. I scoop up the magazine clips and stuff them in my pocket. "I'll ask my mom if she can take us to the store."

"You don't have a seamstress?"

Imitating Odelia at her stuffiest, I say, "No. Today, we shall have to make do with what's available at the Porchtown clothing suppliers." Inside I cannot control myself because I'm thinking: *Wait until Odelia sees the mall!!*

The Princess's New Clothes

Mom beeps the horn, and we climb into her favorite ride—an antique Volkswagen bus with a humongous peace sign on the side. Mom understands how I feel about that VW. She knows why I slouch in the middle seat. She knows why I beg to be dropped off a quarter-mile away from school or any other place. She knows I cannot be seen in this totally uncool excuse for transportation.

The Porchtown Mall is not a huge mall by any standard. It has two department stores with a main floor and a second floor. That's it. Mom says I can spend sixty bucks. She's probably sold more crafts than usual this week. When she scores extra cash, she's generous with it.

Odelia and I take off for the first store. Mom soon gets lost in her own world, chatting to the mannequins about burlap sacks and love beads. We stay far enough ahead of her so no one can tell she's with us.

Weaving our way through the crowd, Odelia is quiet and reserved. She walks like a scared kitty beside me and is skittish when another person comes within a foot of her. The sheer number of clothes, purses, accessories, and snacks sends her into shock. I've lost count of how many times she asked me if we lived in the wealthiest city in the land. Give it up already, Odelia. I can't believe there are no places like this where she is from.

We duck in and out of stores, studying designer, vintage, and retro fashions. We settle on a store with a huge 50% OFF sign and go in.

"What about this?" I ask Odelia as I step out of the dressing room. I'm in a black razorback tank with I HAVE ENOUGH FRIENDS splashed across the chest. I've paired it with destroyed, black wash, super skinny jeans and a gray belt with silver studs.

"It's horrid," Odelia replies. "Someone needs to repair those pants. How's this?" She's in a Hawaiian-print sundress that screams tourist. A flower scrunchie is perched on her hair like a tiara.

"Time to weed the garden," I say, shooting the scrunchie across the store like an elastic band.

Next, we pick out outfits for each other, hoping we'll be forced out of our comfort zones. Odelia chooses green camouflage cargos for me and a tan fake-leather jacket. She makes me try on a tank top with polka dots on it, and I like that they clash with everything else. No one needs to be too matchy-matchy.

I pick out a black tiered mini and a white shirt with an asymmetrical neckline for Odelia. Add to that a chunky chain necklace, two thick black bangles, and a purse painted with skulls, and all telltale signs of princess-ness melt away.

We haul our bags to the bus. I'm beat, but Odelia's got enough energy left to scribble furiously in her ODELIA'S GUIDE TO THE SOCIAL GRACES notebook. She better not whip out a lesson while we're stuck in traffic.

Mom asks Odelia, "Would you like to stay for dinner, dear? We're having oyster stew."

"I appreciate the invitation, Mrs. Baransky. I would love to."

"You have charming manners, Odelia. Maybe your polite behavior will rub off on our Bernice." Mom parks her sunglasses on her perm and shoots me a look in the rearview mirror.

Wait a sec. I'm not polite?

"My godmother is a firm believer in proper social graces," Odelia tells my mom. "In fact, I've been teaching Bern—"

"Hey, Mom! Watch out for the geese!" I yell. There's not a goose in sight. But I don't want Odelia filling Mom in on what we're up to. I don't want anyone to learn about these lessons. So far, the results have been less than newsworthy anyway. After what happened at the park, my chances with Wyatt probably equal my ability to make a clean half-pipe run. Meaning, zero.

"Mrs. Baransky, thank you for the invitation. I must first ask my godmother." Then Odelia turns to me. "May I please borrow your telephone, Bernice?"

I watch Odelia struggle with my phone, and then I help her get connected to Serena. Their conversation is short. Odelia's allowed to stay for dinner.

After dinner, Odelia slips into the living room to make more notes in that notebook of hers. I can only imagine what I did, or didn't do, that served as inspiration for four pages of intense scribbling. Odelia doesn't fill me in or start a new lesson. When we say our good-byes, I make her promise to give the new clothes a try.

I slip into a crocheted afghan and curl up on the couch to digest the oysters swimming in my gut. I want to catch up on a book that's on my summer reading list. It's *Stargirl* by Jerry Spinelli, and I can totally relate to the main character. When my eyes get tired, I spend an hour obsessing over middle school and whether or not I'll fit in. Stargirl didn't fit in at first, then she did, and then she didn't. I'm at the part where her cheerleaders have given up on her. To them, different turned out to be not cool. Has Wyatt decided I'm too different? Maybe that's why he was laughing at me.

Thinking about Wyatt forces me to remember that the skate-off is less than a month away. If I can't get kick flips and a half-pipe trick down, I'll have to bail.

I fall asleep to the sound of Mom and Dad murmuring in the kitchen. In my dream, they've changed into talking doggies . . .

"We love her," Dad says. "Nothing will change that. However, we owe her the truth."

"Remember how she came to us on a sweltering hot day like today?" Mom asks. "We opened the door after hearing that helpless cry, and there she was cuddled in a pink blanket in a basket. I fell in love with her that very moment."

"Righteous, hon."

"No one will take her away, will they?"

"No, that's not possible."

I shake myself out of my sleep, get up, and stumble into the kitchen. I pour a glass of milk, put two chocolate chip cookies on a plate, and plop down on a kitchen chair.

"There's our sleepy sweetie," Mom says.

"I had the weirdest dream about you guys," I say. I fill them in on what I heard in my sleep.

Mom looks at Dad. Dad looks at Mom. I wrap the afghan around me tighter. "What's the matter?"

"How about that?" Dad says. "You had a *dream* we were—"

Mom interrupts. "Cute little puppies!" Mom smoothes out a damp curl that got plastered to my cheek while I was napping. "Ruff!"

Dad takes in the whole mother-daughter moment. He adds, "And the way you're snuggled in that afghan, you look—"

"You look well rested," Mom say. "What's happening at the skate park these days? Can you tell us more about that competition?"

My parents never linger on a single subject, which I appreciate. I don't appreciate a lot of their quirks, especially how they finish each other's sentences, but I'm used to it. I answer Mom, "It's the Lawrence County Skate-Off. I can do almost all of the required tricks, but I still need practice."

"Right on," Dad says.

Mom nods. "Perhaps Odelia can help?"

"I doubt that. Odelia's new to skating."

"She's a unique gal, isn't she? Maybe a bit odd?"

These are questions I don't really have to answer, right?

"Anywho," Mom continues, "I'm glad you've found a new friend, Bernice. But I have been curious about one thing."

Fiddlesticks. Here comes the part where Mom asks why Odelia dresses the way she does, and why we had to make an emergency trip to the mall.

16

A Classic Failure Tale

Three days have gone by and Mom hasn't bugged me anymore about Odelia. That night after dinner, she only asked me to collect twigs from the yard so she could add them to her latest craft project—stick figure angels. I'm grateful that Mom's deepest thoughts involve inanimate objects.

My cell rings, and I pick it up. Roxanne's on the other end. "We should hang out at Winnie's. I want to see that boy you know. You were supposed to tell me when he shows up at the park so I could go there, and you never did."

"I got busy," I tell her.

"Maybe he'll show up at Winnie's today. Let's go. Pick you up in five."

"I have to work at Smile Academy till noon," I tell Roxanne. "It's volunteer work, so I'm out of extra icy money. And my mom just spent a ton on me at the mall, so I can't ask her for more."

"Let's go anyway. My treat," Roxanne says. "Meet me there after lunch." She hangs up.

It bugs me that Roxanne hasn't even given me a choice. I want a choice! I call her back and say, "I don't want to go to Winnie's. I need to practice tricks for the Lawrence County Skate-Off. I was planning to skate until dinner, and Wyatt and I are—"

"Excuse me," Roxanne interrupts with a nasty tone. "I didn't realize that you two had plans."

"Give it a rest," I tell her. "I told you. Nothing's going on between us." Roxanne has no idea how much nothing, *nothing* is.

"All right already," Roxanne says, calming down. "Listen, my mom will find time to drill me on those lines for the commercial if I stick around my house. Can I come over before you leave for the park? I want you to watch me do a reverse French braid on my hair, and tell me if it turns out like in the picture. It won't take long. It'll be great!"

"Sure," I say, without enthusiasm.

"And then maybe I can follow you to the park?"

"Whatever."

We hang up. I get dressed for camp by tossing on my polka dot tank. I add the navy flats. They're the cleanest shoes I've owned in forever, complete with clean starchy bows and shiny bronze stars. I peek at myself in my bedroom mirror, and the girl staring back at me is . . . well, she practically looks like a middle-schooler. I'm reminded of the fun time I had at the mall with Odelia. I hope she wears her new clothes today, too.

I arrive at camp at ten. Odelia's already there, with her new outfit on! What possessed her to add a sparkly headband that's as close to a tiara as you can get, I. Have. No. Idea.

The campers call out my name and when things settle down, Nellie pulls me over. "Nellie Frances O'Malley and Bernice are BFFs!"

I nod and sit with her. She picks up a fat pencil, then puts it down. She takes my face in her hands and stares at me, exactly like she did the first day we met.

"What's wrong?" I ask. I wonder if a boogie is lurking in my nose or if that zit that's been hiding behind a thin curtain of skin has decided to make its debut.

Nellie squints one eye, then the other. "Bernice is boo-ti-ful," she says. "Very, very, very bootiful."

My cheeks feel warm. Lately, I've been changing cheek colors faster than a chameleon. And chameleons are not beautiful.

I blow my nose in a tissue. I pick at my cheek. No zit. Nellie puts her concentration back into writing. She practices the same numbers until they are perfect. Twos and fives are hard for her, yet she doesn't give up. When I get on that half-pipe again, I'm channeling Nellie. Nellie is not a quitter.

Miss Robyn notices how well I get along with Nellie, so she assigns me to Robbie and Claire's project—building a tower out of cardboard boxes. The big ones go at the bottom, the small ones at the top. It's supposed to help with Robbie and Claire's coordination. Miss Robyn also mentions it'll help with their interpersonal skills. I have no idea what she means.

Every time Claire and I stack a box, Robbie knocks the tower down.

"Robbie, we can't do this if you keep destroying what we've built," I tell him.

Robbie shows me his meanest face. "Robbie is Destroyer Man. Robbie is Destroyer Man." He kicks the boxes across the room.

I gather up the boxes and start again. Claire balances one on top of the other. This isn't easy for her. Her vision stinks, and those thick glasses she wears don't seem to work that great.

Seconds later—WHAM! Robbie knocks the tower down again. "Robbie is Destroyer Man."

Claire's glasses get foggy. "No!" she cries.

I quickly reset the boxes. Claire takes off her glasses and wipes her drippy eyes on her sleeve.

Robbie hits the boxes again! They fly everywhere.

Claire screams. "Tower! My tower!"

I can't take this. Seriously. "Stop it, Robbie. Stop knocking down the tower!"

"Destroyer Man! Destroyer Man!" Robbie jumps on a box, smashing it flat.

"That's it!" I yell, tugging on Robbie's arm above the elbow. "You are not Destroyer Man! Now, get over here and start acting normal."

As soon as those words leave my lips, I feel dizzy with regret. Robbie will never be normal, at least in the way I think normal is normal. I back away. My blood feels like it has left my body.

Miss Robyn is at my side. "Bernice, please come with me."

I shoot a glance at Odelia. She's grumbling under her breath like Mom and Dad do when they're about to lecture me for doing something stupid. Every boy, girl, and camp counselor stares at me as I leave the room.

Once inside Miss Robyn's office, I sit and bite a hangnail. I feel terrible. I am a terrible person. I know what's coming. I'm getting fired. I *should* get fired. I am worse than terrible. I should be arrested.

"What happened in there was unacceptable," Miss Robyn says, pacing around her office. "You need to monitor what you say." Miss Robyn slaps her hands down on her desk, and I jump.

"I just lost it," I say, not really offering an explanation.

With less of a harsh tone Miss Robyn adds, "I'm at fault, as well. I should never have put you in that situation with Robbie and Claire." She paces around the room and flips a pencil through her fingers like a baton. "You're usually such a good role model. I know it's hard to process this, but you are about the same age as many of the campers, and it's good for them to be around you. They look up to you, Bernice." Miss Robyn sighs. "But you are a work-in-progress yourself. You have lots to learn."

"I'll make it up to Robbie. I won't come back tomorrow."

"Please do that."

I feel sick—throw-up-faint-dead-away sick. I get up to go.

Miss Robyn continues. "Let's both take a deep breath and sit. Let me be clear. We are returning to the playroom where I want you to apologize to Robbie loud enough for every camper to hear. In the future, remember your manners. If you had used a calmer tone and said 'Please,' Robbie might have responded differently."

"In the future?"

"Yes," Miss Robyn replies. "Stay on as a volunteer. *Please* stay. The kids love having you here."

"I like being here," I mumble.

When I find Robbie, I stoop down so we're eye-to-eye, and tell him I'm sorry. He puts his pudgy hands on my shoulders and plants a soggy smooch on my forehead. My heart swells.

I get back to our tower. "Robbie, can you put this box on top of mine and leave it there? Please?" Robbie cocks his head, picks up a box, and puts it in place. Next, Claire balances her box on top of Robbie's. She shoots Robbie a deadly don't-you-dare look.

Robbie walks around the tower. I can feel his tension building.

"Hey, Robbie, when we're finished, we get to glue all the boxes together. Won't that be fun?"

Robbie takes off "flying" for the supply shelf, yelling. "Robbie is Glue Man! Robbie is Glue Man!"

I'm relieved that Robbie is now a superhero instead of a destroyer.

I leave Smile Academy and ride home. It's been a tough morning. I can't wait to go skateboarding. Roxanne meets me at my front door and reminds me about my meeting with Roxy, Super Stylist to the Stars.

"I'll French braid mine first, then yours," she says. "Since yours is shorter and layered, it'll be the challenge I need."

It's taking Roxanne forever to get her braid done, so I beg her to skip mine. I need to get out of here. I need to get to the park!

"Hey, Bernie, you know what? I told my mom I didn't want to do any more commercials."

Here we go. It's all about Roxanne. But I listen. She *is* my best friend, one of my only friends. I have to remember that.

"Mom said I can't quit. Get this, the money I make goes into an account to pay for my college. What if I don't want to go to college? What if I want to go to cosmetology school?"

I'm guessing that a cosmetology school is a beauty school, but I can't be sure. Whatever it is, no one decides their career in middle school. I wipe the deck of my skateboard with an old sock then rub the dust and dirt off of the bottom. Roxanne keeps braiding and re-braiding her hair and yakking nonstop about her favorite subject: Roxanne.

"I have to go to New York again tomorrow. My mom wants me to try out for a toothpaste commercial. I hate these auditions. I get nervous. Unbelievably nervous. Wouldn't you be nervous, Bernie? BERNIE? Are you even listening to me?"

That's it. I've had it. I slap my board down on the floor and shove it in Roxanne's direction. "I'm tired of hearing you complain! Get over yourself. Do something about it. Get your mom to listen to you!"

That shut her up. Finally.

"I'm outta here," I tell Roxanne, picking up my skate gear. "I've had a bad day. And news flash! I have things going on that You. Would. Not. Believe."

I storm out of my bedroom, run down the stairs, and leave through the front door. Roxanne stomps out behind me. I walk to the right, toward the skate park. She walks left. We don't say good-bye, but Roxanne calls out, "You're a jerk."

In a Small Village Park

I have to get myself to the park, and fast. I don't care if Wyatt's there or not. I need to pound some pavement.

But the second I see Wyatt beyond the gate, I shrink. I can't roll around him. I can't avoid him. If my skateboard had magical powers, I'd ask it to make me invisible.

"Yo, Dude," he calls. "I've got the sickest trick for you for the half. You up for it?"

"Um . . . wait . . ." Complete sentences are impossible, and to myself I say, *I'm sorry I'm letting you down, Odelia!*

I find my courage and look Wyatt straight in the eye. "Why did you laugh at me the other day?"

"What?" Wyatt ollies his board. Twice. Is he nervous or is he just practicing?

Odelia's lesson, the Art of Crafty Conversation, sneaks into my brain. *Speak your mind.* I take a deep breath. In and out. And let it rip. "The last time I saw you, you were here with friends, over there." I nod toward the fence. "You were making fun of me because . . . I was . . ."

Fiddlesticks! This is harder than I ever thought. I yank my helmet off and tuck my hair behind my ears. I dig my heel into the ground. "Were you laughing at me because I was hanging with the kids from Smile Academy?"

"What kids? Smile Academy? What's that? A school? There's nothin' funny about summer school, Dude."

"Smile Academy is a summer *camp* for Down syndrome kids. I know the campers."

"Hey, that's cool," Wyatt says, popping a third ollie.

No drama? I was expecting drama. Wyatt seems fine with the campers. "You weren't making fun of me?"

"Dude! No! Zeke, Troy, and me—we were watching the old guy shred. It was hysterical."

"Yeah, he's pretty funny," I say, relieved.

Wyatt agrees. He rolls away, skating to the top of the nine-stair hubba. He easily ollies up the slanted concrete slab and grinds his way down.

I roll over there and watch. I want to keep the conversation going. I want to tell him what I do at the academy. But part of me worries that Wyatt will see volunteer work as a waste of precious skate time. Despite Odelia's advice about crafty conversation, I move to keep my fat mouth shut. And simply escape. "Later," I say, pushing off toward the manny pad to perfect my 50-50.

About twenty minutes go by before Wyatt pulls up next to me. "The trick for the half-pipe, remember? I want to show you one. C'mon!"

"Right," I say. I sound all calm and casual, but I'm totally freaking out with happiness. Wyatt still wants to help me!

As we skate over to the half, Wyatt asks, "You can do a rock to fakie, can't you?"

I nod. "Only on the quarter. It's my fave." I ask him what his favorite trick is, even though I figured that out ages ago.

Wyatt answers, "Front nose manual."

Odelia is wrong. Crafty conversation is not like chess. It's like the game of Twenty Questions. No, a game of One Question. That ends in twenty seconds.

Wyatt rides hard and fast on the half-pipe. When he gets to the other side, he presses on the back of his board so that the front trucks and wheels pop over the coping and the middle balances on it. Then he turns his shoulders and does a 180. Next, like it's no big deal, he rolls down.

"It's a rock and roll," he explains. "After that pivot, you hang out on the coping for a couple of seconds before you go back down."

I pretend that I understand and can handle it. Truth is, I'm so torn up inside, I feel like an emergency trip to the rec center portable potty might be a good idea.

Wyatt rolls away and does it again. He pulls off the trick as easily as a pro skater. "You're up," he says.

"I just learned to drop in. Getting up the other side, doing a trick, and coming back down?" I shrug a shoulder. Sweat is pouring out from every pore. My pits are Niagara Falls. I'm extremely grateful for the dots on my tank top that help hide the wet stains.

Wyatt gives me a friendly push. "Do it, Dude."

I walk up to the top of the half-pipe, adjust my elbow pad, and switch knee pads. I take off my helmet, untwist the buckle, and put it on again.

"GO!" Wyatt yells.

I scan the bleachers for Odelia or my mighty munchkins. No cheerleaders. I'm on my own. I'm not sure if that's a good thing or a bad thing. I jump on my board and drop in. My practice has paid off. This part I can do. I roll up the other side, a little farther than the midway point, and pull off a clean kick turn.

"Faster!" Wyatt yells. "You've gotta go faster. Don't turn. You've gotta bang those trucks over the coping."

"Get ready to call 9-1-1," I shout. On the next run, I pump my legs harder on the drop. I'm going fast. Too fast! I'm about to fly over the coping!

Luckily, the steep upside slows me down to the best possible speed, and I go for it. I pop up the front wheels, but when I rotate, my butt rotates to the ground. THUD! Wyatt asks if I need help. I signal to him that I don't. I shake off the pain, and take off to try again. After another fall, I tell him to not waste any more time on me and to go practice his own moves for the skate-off. I'm proud of myself for speaking the "song of my heart," as Odelia puts it. Wyatt leaves and once I'm alone, I can finally breathe normally again.

After ten tries, I'm really good at getting the nose over. After fifteen, I get my deck on the coping, but can't get that 180 down for the re-entry. So frustrating! I have had enough. I am exhausted. I am sore. I am thirsty. I have a bloody nose. And the zit I felt earlier has decided it is show-time. "Fiddlesticks!" I rip off my helmet, stretch out the kinks in my legs and arms, and search for Wyatt. He's not anywhere inside the park. Then I spot him. He's sitting on bleachers. With Roxanne.

I slap the tail end of my board against the ground and kick it up into my hand. I walk home. Alone.

Queen for a Day

The next day, I find Odelia sitting on my sliding board, waving her pink notebook at me. "Hi, Bernice," she calls.

"No more worthless lessons," I say. "They don't matter anymore. *Wyatt* doesn't matter anymore. He'd rather be friends with Roxanne."

"My lessons aren't worthless and Wyatt *does* matter. As for Roxanne, she's the girl I saw you with at Winnie's?"

"That's her. Be glad you don't know her. We are . . . we *were* best friends, but she officially met Wyatt yesterday, and I found them on the bleachers having a crafty conversation of their own."

"They could've been chatting about the weather for all you know, Bernice."

"I know. I'm not mad at him. It's actually Roxanne who's been getting on my nerves lately. I'm tired of hearing about her life. Tired of having my world revolve around hers."

"Maybe that's why she values your friendship," Odelia says. "She needs you. You are everything she's not. I think she talks about herself because she seeks your approval."

Dr. Odelia should have her own show. But what she's saying makes sense. I have it good compared to Roxanne. My parents let me do what I like to do; they never make me feel bad about myself. Except for that time in the VW when Mom commented about Odelia's politeness rubbing off on me, but that was nothing. My parents don't nag. Roxanne's mom is a pain in the butt.

Odelia is snapping her fingers at me. "Let's move on. I've been making notes and have found a flaw we must work on."

I put my head in my hands. "Another flaw? That's. Just. Great."

Odelia holds up the notebook. She taps on a page:

"ODELIA'S GUIDE TO THE SOCIAL GRACES
LESSON 7: MANNERS

OBJECTIVE: Bernice will understand the importance of manners and how the use of manners at home, school, and other social settings will diminish her awkwardness. (Note to self: Bernice's manners, or lack thereof, leaves a taste of vinegar in one's mouth.)"

Odelia runs up the sliding board and stands on the platform. "Attention! Attention! Queen Odelia reigns supreme. Ye must listen to the queen."

"You're not the Queen of Porchtown."

"Ha! All princesses become queens." Odelia stands, chin held high. "Are you practicing what you've learned?"

I shade my eyes from the sun and call up to the queen. "I think about you and those lessons a lot. I was a real charmer around Wyatt until Roxanne showed up."

Odelia studies her notebook. "As I stated, our lesson today is on manners."

"I've got enough manners," I say defiantly. "I'm not a please-and-thank-you person. But I'm not rude." In a flash, I replay what happened with Robbie yesterday, and think twice about what I spit out to Odelia.

"Manners don't come naturally to you, Bernice. Let's review the proper use of please and thank you. There have been times when you should have said these words."

"I'm not a four-year-old. I don't need a lesson fit for a preschooler." I plop on a swing, pull back on the chains, lift my feet and stay there, staring at the sky. I am totally a four-year-old sometimes.

Odelia tosses a paper to me. She has written down every time I've forgotten to say please since we've met. There are ten entries. Another list shows the five times I've forgotten to thank somebody, and those bodies include my parents, Miss Robyn, the cashier lady at the mall, and a couple of other people I never thought to say thank you to. Odelia also points out that I forgot to say I'm sorry a couple of times. She brings up Robbie, and reminds me I didn't say I'm sorry to him until after Miss Robyn reamed me out. I can work on manners, I guess.

"You'll catch more flies with honey than with vinegar," Odelia tells me.

"What in the world does that mean?"

"It means that people will respond more favorably if you treat them with respect. Make manners a part of your personality. Practice at Smile Academy with the children. Practice at the skate park. Practice at home. Thank your parents for the home they've provided, the delicious meals, etc. Practice with me."

"With you?"

Odelia taps her foot. I notice her flip flops—nice leather ones like they sell in the skate and surf stores. I want a pair, but they're fifty bucks.

"Where did you get them?" I ask. "They're awesome."

"Do you mean my flipper flops? I saw a picture of these in a magazine and had them made."

"They're flip flops," I correct her. "Are you saying that you have a personal shoemaker that goes along with your personal seamstress and personal carpenter?"

"Yes," Odelia answers. "Collin is my shoemaker. We have an entire staff who live in small cottages on the mansion's property – a seamstress, carpenter, butler, cook, maid, stable manager, and a few more. We brought them with us when we moved here. They're wonderful! Collin is especially talented. His workmanship exceeds anything in any store. Serena and I returned to the mall to make sure his were as good."

The extra mall trip explains the rest of Odelia's outfit—a logo-free, light-pink pocketed tee, classic boyfriend jeans, and a leather belt that matches her "flipper flops." The tiara is officially gone. Her hair is down. Pinned behind one ear is a black barrette with red, orange, pink, and green stones.

"Focus, Bernice," Odelia says.

"I was admiring your clothes. And that barrette. Where did you get it?"

Odelia pulls out the barrette and throws it to me. "I made it," she says. "You can have it."

"I, um, don't know what to say." I pull on a random curl that I missed when straightening my hair this morning.

"Exactly," Odelia reprimands. "You should have immediately said thank you. And this is why you need lesson seven. Let's begin. I'll demonstrate." Odelia clears her throat. A long speech is coming. "Thank you for showing me around my new neighborhood, and for introducing me to the skate park and the mall. Thank you for allowing me to volunteer with you. Thank you for showing me how to be more easygoing. Thanks for . . ." Odelia stops. She bites her lip. "Thank you for your friendship, Bernice."

"You're thanking *me*?" I ask.

"Yes. Now, let me hear you."

"Please, *please* can we *not* do this lesson?"

Odelia raises that left eyebrow. She makes circles with her arms, encouraging me to keep going. Part of me hopes she'll lose her balance and take a nose dive off the slide.

"Thank you for showing me I can be next to a boy without making a fool out of myself. Almost. Thank you for helping me see that I can be a girl without being a girly girl. Almost. Thank you for coming to Smile Academy because I didn't want to go at first and having you along made it easier. Thank you for showing me how to walk, talk, and maybe not end up a total loser. Thank you for . . . for being my friend." I bow to Odelia, queen of my sliding board.

"That was nice, Bernice," Odelia says. She slides down, straightens up, and tucks a finger under my chin. She tries to look very serious, but a giggle sneaks out as she says loudly, "Arise, oh worthy one. It's time for my other notes."

Odelia's other notes are five pages long. When she's finished drilling me on "appropriate etiquette," we leave my yard and chill in the AC in my room. Odelia doesn't come up with another lesson, which I appreciate.

Then, out of the blue, she says, "Serena sold Prince Chancellor Pomegranate a saddle. When he came to pick it up, he asked to see me. He was really nervous. He kept picking at his ear. I thought a ball of earwax might pop out! I wanted to talk to him, alone, so I took him for a stroll in the garden. When we finished, I challenged him to a race to the end of the property. It was okay. No, I mean, it was great! He told me he never expected that. Can you imagine that? He liked that I was sporty! He wants to teach me *his* favorite sport—archery. I haven't told Serena, for she would be chilly about this."

"She would not be *chill*," I correct her. "You're going to shoot a bow and arrow? I'd pay to see that."

"I will be wonderful. I will be full of awe with myself."

"Awesome."

"Oh, yes! Awesome!" Odelia spins herself across my lawn, out to the street, and up her driveway. She is one weirdo girl, with or without the princess gown and tiara. But there might be hope for her yet.

An Invitation to the Ball

Today, Smile Academy is a zoo. I'm filling in as story time person because Odelia is two hours away learning archery from Chance. I've read every Dr. Seuss book in the camp's library, and my voice is completely hoarse.

Jessica finds the bag of marshmallows reserved for s'mores, eats them all, and throws up on the window. Easy to see she had oatmeal and raisins for breakfast. Gross! Joe comes in late because he's broken his finger—his middle finger. He holds it up for us to check out. Angelo falls asleep while hiding during Hide 'N Seek, and we can't find him for fifteen minutes. Nellie is not her usual chatty self, and Miss Robyn tells me she's upset. Mrs. O'Malley has lost her job, and she can't afford to send Nellie to camp any longer. This is the worst part of my day yet!

Nellie and I play a game of Checkers. She beats me, but that still doesn't cheer her up. I challenge her to a funny face competition, hoping that'll make her feel better. We aren't sure of the winner, but both of us end up in a much better mood. I love hanging out with Nellie. When she stops coming to camp, I will miss her so much.

Before I leave, Miss Robyn hands me a note. "It's about a prince and princess party we're having next Tuesday," she says. "It's Nellie's last day. Mrs. O'Malley tells me Nellie's been in an awful state. She doesn't understand why she has to leave. I thought it would be nice to make her last day one she'll always remember. We'll have tea and cake, wear costumes, and turn this place into a castle with all the trimmings. Can you and Odelia come dressed up as princesses?"

"Sure," I tell Miss Robyn. "I'd do anything to make Nellie happy. When I was little, dressing like a princess was my favorite thing to do, so sure, I can figure out a way to do that. And Odelia definitely won't have a problem with it."

"Perfect," Miss Robyn says, and hustles back to her office.

After the kids are settled in for lunch, I change out of my navy flats and cruise to the park. I hope Miss Robyn brings the kids here later. They could use more outdoor time. A little exercise wouldn't hurt, either.

Porchtown Skate Park is more crowded than I've ever seen it. Word has gotten out about the skate-off and every eleven- to fourteen-year-old in the county who owns a skateboard is here. I am not good at *not* colliding with other skaters when it's this crazy. Twice I've smacked into somebody. Twice I've actually gotten up the guts to say I'm sorry. The first kid ignored my terrific manners; the second had lots to say to me. If Dad ever heard me swearing like that, he'd dunk me in the bay.

I swerve in and out of the obstacles, roll up and down the volcano, and find a space to practice the tricks for the skate-off. My kick-flip is still sketchy. I land it eighty percent of the time. Seventy percent is more like it. Not bad odds. I finish a couple more runs and grinds on random things, collapse on my board, and look over at the half-pipe. I swear it's grown.

"Dude, don't let it intimidate you. Or the kids dominating it. You master the rock and roll yet?"

Wyatt. His voice makes me feel gooey inside like skateboard wax that's been left out in the sun. I picture him talking to Roxanne and it kills my confidence. "Nope, but I will. Are you ready?" Listen to me, all inquisitive and mannerly, at least on the outside. On the inside, I'm wondering why Wyatt was hanging out with Roxanne. They have nothing in common!

"Looking forward to it," Wyatt says. "There's some local band playing that day."

"No Boys Allowed," I say.

"What?" Wyatt asks, scrunching up his face.

"That's the name of the band." I want to smirk, but he'll think I'm making fun of him.

Wyatt takes it all in. "Cool."

News flash! The boy is staring at me. I don't know how to act. I don't know what else to say. I want to ask about Roxanne, but that's impossible.

"See ya around," I mumble. And then I remember: *Manners do not come naturally to you . . .* and I blurt out, "Thank you for helping me the other day. You're a really great skater."

Wyatt runs his hand through his sun-streaked hair. He doesn't say a word. I don't say a word. I can hear a clock in my brain ticking off each awkward second. Do I leave first? Do I wait for him to leave?

Wyatt turns away, but turns back. "Dude, I've got competition. *You* rock, too."

Wyatt thinks I rock? Wow! My mouth drops open and when I realize how ridiculous I look I change it into a yawn.

"Listen, you wanna come by my house Saturday? Maybe around lunch?" he asks. "I've got a new skate DVD. All the pros are in it. Mega wipeouts. You'd probably like it." Wyatt spins a wheel on his board.

I'm glad that Wyatt thinks I'd like a DVD about professional skaters, huge ramps, impossible verts, and broken bones, but mostly I am in shock. A boy has asked me over!

I swallow hard and squeak out, "Sure." We say good-bye and that's that.

For the rest of the afternoon, I am fearless. I have to push my way in for half-pipe time, and Moron Forge makes things difficult. He constantly blocks my ride. Time to put lesson seven into action again. "Hey, Ron, *please* don't hang at the bottom when you're done. If you don't move, I might crash into you on my next run."

Moron looks up at me. "Berndog, that you?"

"Yeah, it's Bernie." Here we go. It's not like I'm some 170-pound roller derby girl who can body check Moron to the moon. "Please, Ron? I need to practice." I lift my palms to the air, act as adorable as possible, and hope he gets the message. To my utter shock, Moron shrugs, grabs his board, and shuffles off the pipe.

Manners work! But that's not what's important right now. I've got to find Odelia. And fast. I need a lesson on How Not to Act Like an Idiot When I'm at a Boy's House.

Once home, I see Roxanne sitting on my front steps. I've been thinking about Odelia's take on Roxanne, how it makes sense.

"About Wyatt," Roxanne says before I say a word, "when you were busy on your skateboard the other day, he came over to talk to me. But all he did was talk about *you.*"

"What do you mean?" My heart is beating fast like it does right before a big test. If boys are a subject in middle school, I'll fail that class completely.

"He wanted to know where you live, what else you do besides skate. Things like that. Get this, he thought you were *already* in middle school, at Porchtown Catholic or somewhere else. I had to explain that we both just got out of sixth grade and wouldn't be at Porchtown Middle until

September. Embarrassing!"

I blow out a huge sigh. "I bet he's sorry he invited me to his house."

"He did what?" Roxanne shouts.

"He asked me over on Saturday to watch some DVDs. And maybe have lunch."

"See? It doesn't matter that you're a year younger than he is. You'll have a great time. He's really nice." Roxanne fiddles with the edge of her shirt. "Bernie, I'm sorry for calling you a jerk. Still friends?"

I can't stay mad at Roxanne, so I apologize, too. I want to be finished with the drama. "Sure," I say. "And FYI, I'm just another skater to Wyatt. That's it."

Roxanne gets up. "Sounds like he'd like to get to know the girl who hides inside that skater." She pats me on the back like I'm a faithful golden retriever. "I see a boy from my church on the corner. I'm going to try and catch up to him. Think about what I said."

As if I could possibly think of anything else.

Be Our Guest

In the morning, I call Odelia and tell her to get over here pronto and shoot me whatever lessons I need to get through tomorrow at Wyatt's. We'll be away from the park, so it's my chance to make a different impression. A better impression. I need to know what to do when I meet his mom, how I should act, what I should say! And then there's lunch. I'll have to eat in front of him! Dang.

Odelia doesn't waste any time. She's clearly excited about her mission to make me into the perfect guest. She pulls out that pink notebook. It's showing some serious signs of wear and tear. Odelia reads:

"ODELIA'S GUIDE TO THE SOCIAL GRACES

LESSON 8: A GRACIOUS GUEST IS NOT A GHASTLY GUEST

OBJECTIVE: Bernice will learn to present herself
as a well-groomed, respectful, and gracious guest. (Note to self: Serena has
cursed the day that mud ended up on her rug, compliments of not-so-
respectful Bernice, who wore filthy sneakers into our parlor.)"

"My mom tries to get me to leave my sneaks outside. I always forget. I'm sorry. Did I ruin your carpet?"

"No, you didn't. Serena exaggerates. I am so happy, however, that you've apologized. I have chosen this example to emphasize how much you still have to learn. When you enter someone's home, please be neat and wipe your feet. If your shoes are horribly dirty, take them off."

"Easy enough. What else?"

"If you're wearing a coat and the host does not ask to take it, either leave it on, or place it on a chair."

"How about a hoodie? What if it's cool tomorrow and I wear a hoodie, but inside it's burning hot? If I don't have the chance to get rid of it, sweat will drip from my earlobes, neck, and a bunch of other places. I'll end up looking like a swamp monster, and my hair will frizz!"

"Use a deodorant and frizzy control spray. If you keep your hoodie on, think cold thoughts. If you remove it, don't leave it for Wyatt's parent to pick up."

"You mean his mother. His mom! What do I say to her?"

Odelia rubs her temple. I'm giving her a workout. She opens her notebook to GENUINE GREETINGS. "Review this."

I review. Talking to random people is one thing. Talking to Wyatt's mom is another. I pace and think, and try to get a grip. I desperately want to be one of those kids who can get through social situations without feeling sick.

Odelia yaks on and on about how I shouldn't touch anything in Wyatt's house, and how I should be careful not to "knock over any knick knacks." What in the world is a knick knack and why would I knick a knack? She tells me I should make polite conversation with Wyatt's little sister and his mom, but not get too nosy. "Speak only when spoken to," Odelia commands.

"What if I have to go to the bathroom?" I ask, because I need to know how to escape if I can't hold it in. And I can never hold it in. Mom says I have the bladder of a gerbil.

Odelia walks around me, thinking. "Tell someone, of course."

"If I tell Wyatt I have to pee, I'll sound like his little sister!"

Odelia clicks her tongue. "No, you won't. You'll figure out how to say it so that you sound like you."

Great. One thing I've already figured out is that Odelia's answer is no help to me whatsoever.

Odelia moves on to the next lesson, and says:

"ODELIA'S GUIDE TO THE SOCIAL GRACES

LESSON 9: THE TABLE FABLE

OBJECTIVE: Bernice will learn basic table etiquette. Like Aesop, I shall tell a tale of table manners in the hope that the lesson becomes clear. (Note to self: Bernice enjoys eating on the run, and she often resembles an energetic, voracious monkey.)"

I ignore the bit about being a monkey because . . . well, I do eat in a hurry, and I'm always starving. "It's story time?"

"Listen to this short fable: A young woman is invited for lunch at a neighbor's house. She arrives and sits down, but never eats a single morsel. Therefore, she dies. The end. Why do you suppose she never ate?"

"She wasn't hungry?"

Odelia shakes her head.

"She didn't like what the neighbor was serving?"

Odelia shakes her head harder.

"Wait!" I say. "She had to pee!"

Odelia laughs, but then turns on a stern expression. "Why didn't she eat? Why didn't she leave?"

"She was a prisoner?"

Odelia's a temperamental badger stomping her foot. "Come on, Bernice. Think!"

"Someone's royal manners are absent," I say. "Believe me, I don't have a clue why this person starved to death. Not. A. Clue."

"She was waiting for the neighbor, also known as the host, to begin eating first, as is customary. But the host had an emergency and had to leave, so no one began to eat. And, the woman never asked to be excused from the table."

"What a lame story. I'd never do those things."

Odelia ignores me and makes a list of other things I'd never do, but might think about doing if I'm a guest. Like, putting my napkin on my lap, passing food to the right, taking small bites, chewing with my mouth closed. Oh, and forget about burping and putting my elbows on the table.

Finally, Odelia shows me how to cut meat, scoop up veggies, eat a sandwich without making a mess, and how I should ask to be excused. Excuse me! This is too much information. I'll need to take a cheat sheet with me to Wyatt's!

A Damsel in Distress

I'm walking, not skating, to Wyatt's house. I can't risk wrecking my hair—hair that I straightened for two hours last night and re-straightened for an hour this morning. When I called Roxanne to tell her I was getting ready, she ran over to seal my 'do with her mega-hold hairspray. A hurricane couldn't dent it.

Odelia strolls next to me. I fill her in about the prince and princess party Miss Robyn has planned and her eyes twinkle like the jewels in her missing tiara.

"Wear a princess gown and every accessory you can dig up. Especially your tiara," I say. "Tell the kids stories of castles and moats, and witches, and your godmother—make Serena a *fairy* godmother. That's more interesting. Let's see what else. You can talk about Magnifico, Collin the shoemaker, your snooty butler, and all those other people who sound like they're part of a fairy tale. Everybody loves a good story."

"Serena, Magnifico, Collin, and Gerard are not characters from a book. They are real. And Gerard is not snooty. He's actually cool."

"Listen to you," I say. "You sound like me."

"But *you* will look like *me* for the party. I'll bring a lovely gown over Tuesday morning—a gown that is perfect for you. Maybe one in peach or pale yellow. No . . . rose. It must be rose, offset with a white satin sash. You will be the belle of the ball."

"A rosy dress to match my rosy middle name," I tell her. "It's Rose."

"Your middle name is Rose?" Odelia asks. "My middle name is Rose as well!"

"No way!" I say. "We have matching middle names."

"How fun! But *you* will be the one in the rosy gown." Odelia claps her hands together in excitement.

"Hey, Odelia *Rose*, Wyatt's house is coming up. You should disappear."

Odelia tugs on my arm. "Well, Bernice *Rose*, not before one more important lesson. Listen carefully:

ODELIA'S GUIDE TO THE SOCIAL GRACES
LESSON 10: OODLES OF OOPSIES

OBJECTIVE: Bernice will learn to accept that certain unforeseeable problems are out of her control. She will handle these difficulties with the finesse of a ballerina. (Note to self: The ballerina reference requires quite a stretch of the imagination.)"

"Thanks a lot, Odelia," I spit out sarcastically. "What do you mean by 'unforeseeable problems' and 'difficulties'?"

"Leave your sarcasm at the door," Odelia says. "I'm trying to give you a short lesson *and* lighten your anxious mood. Here we go. Consider quickly how you will act in the following situations. I'll say pass if your answer is acceptable."

"Whatever. Hurry up. We're almost at Wyatt's."

"When you feel a burp coming on, you . . ."

"Run to another room, and burp there."

"Pass. If you spill juice, soda, or food down your shirt, you . . ."

"Run to another room, and turn my shirt inside out."

"Pass. You could politely ask for tonic water and dab the stain."

"When you sneeze and mucus runs out your nose, you . . ."

"Run to find a tissue."

"Pass. If you feel ill and need to vomit . . ."

"Run anywhere there's a sink, toilet, or trash can."

"Pass. But if you are continually running, you will run yourself out of Wyatt's house. Moving on. You have accidentally passed gas *before* getting to the bathroom. You . . ."

"I'd have to move off the planet! Odelia! If that happens, I. Will. Die.

Why are you bringing up these horrible things? What are you trying to do?"

Odelia grins an evil witch grin. "I'm just messing with you," she says. And she runs home.

My nervous frown turns upside down and that smile sticks with me as I walk the rest of the way to Wyatt's. When he opens the door, it's everything I can do to keep from laughing in his face.

There is nothing better in the world than sitting next to a boy you've been in deep like with for weeks. Wyatt has loaded the DVD in the player and for an hour we watch Jake Brown, Ryan Sheckler, and Pierre-Luc Gagnon tear it up. Soon afterward, lunch is ready. It smells more like dinner and my stomach growls. Wyatt didn't hear that, right?

"C'mon, kids," Mrs. Anderson says. "Get the fried chicken while it's hot."

The sight of a chicken leg, deep fried, is usually enough to put me in a food coma. But not today. Today, the drumstick is a UFO, an Unidentified Food Object. I don't know whether to pick it up with my fingers or cut it with a knife. My first thought is: *Odelia, why didn't we cover this!* And my second is: *I have to stall.*

I make a detour for a finger food friendly chip. In that instant, both Wyatt and his mom dive into their drumsticks without the help of a fork. Yay! Problem solved.

Wyatt's Mom is a chatterbox. She asks where I live, how long I've lived on Station Street, what school I go to, and ten more questions. She keeps giving me and Wyatt this motherly look that says *you two are so cute together.* Wyatt is squirming and so am I. Lunch is taking forever. When Mrs. Anderson goes to answer the phone, we get out of there, fast. Around the corner, we both breathe a sigh of relief.

"Sorry about my mom," Wyatt says. We're in his basement and he's popping in a Shaun White skateboard game. "She's not used to seeing me hang with any girls. Girl skaters, I mean. Moose, a.k.a. Mike, Troy, the skinny dude at the park—you've seen him—and Zeke, my best friend, are here more than anybody."

"My friends don't skate," I say, because . . . well, I can't think of anything else to say. I may be getting better at conversation, but sitting on a couch close enough to smell this boy's deodorant has made me forget ninety percent of the English language.

Wyatt says, "You're the only girl I've ever seen there." He hands me one controller, and he takes another.

Once we start skating and competing against each other, we get lost in the game. I'm pretty sure I'm not expected to come up with more than a random "No!" or "Yes!" or "Another game?"

Three hours pass as if by magic. I have to be home by four, so Wyatt walks me upstairs. I make sure to thank Mrs. Anderson and I thank Wyatt, too. Odelia is right. Thank yous don't come naturally to me. How many thank yous did she say I missed? I am not getting called on this again.

Outside, Wyatt fakes intense interest in an empty fast food cup that's by the curb. I say good-bye and start to leave when he gives me a friendly poke in the ribs, and says, "See ya at the park, Bernice."

Wait. A. Minute. He knows my name!

Good thing I left my skateboard home because there's no room for it on the Cloud Nine Express.

You Shall Have a Daughter

Before going up the driveway, I stop by our mailbox for Saturday's mail. There's nothing for me, but one dingy yellow envelope gets my attention. There's no return address and the handwriting looks ancient. Weird.

Mr. and Mrs. George Baransky
PERSONAL AND CONFIDENTIAL
433 Station Street
Porchtown, PA

"Mail's here," I tell Dad. He's leaning over the kitchen sink, filleting very dead, very smelly fish.

"Catch of the day," he says. "Flounders were runnin' this morning."

"Yum. More seafood," I say, without enthusiasm. "Can't we have burgers and fries like every other American? We eat way too much fish. We're messing up the food chain."

"Very funny." Dad chuckles. "I'm expecting a bill for that new freezer I put in the store." He holds up his slimy hands. "Do me a favor and show me the mail? I want to see if it's here."

I lean over the sink and file envelopes one-by-one in front of Dad's eyes. When he sees the envelope with PERSONAL AND CONFIDENTIAL on it, his knife slips.

"OUCH-A-RAMA! I cut my dern finger!" He wipes the blood on a paper towel and draws it up for inspection. "No stitches. Let me have a closer peek at that mail."

He peeks. Then he throws all the mail into the sink with the fish—every envelope except the weird one. "Bern, find your mother for me. Go! Go find her, now!"

Dad hardly ever—no, *never*—orders me around. What's wrong?

Mom is in the garage, walking in circles. "Mr. Sticky? Where are you? I put you down minutes ago to put in a load of laundry and you've disappeared. Please tell me you're not stuck on Miss Scissors again. Are you cutting a rug with her?"

My mother is from a different dimension—a dimension where craft supplies live, breathe, talk, and date each other. "Cutting a rug?" I ask.

"Your grandmother used that term. It means dancing. I'm worried that my glue gun got stuck to the scissors, and they've danced away."

"Got it," I say. "Dad wants you. Right away."

Mom walks over to me. "He's not attempting to make fish meatballs again, is he?"

"No, that's not it. He cut his finger. But what freaked him out was this letter I brought in with the mail. He wants you to come quick."

"What color was the envelope?" Mom asks, her words spilling out in a hurry.

"Yellowish. Looks old."

Mom races out of the garage and into the house as fast as a runner bolting for the finish line. I don't have a clue what is going on with my parents. They're not quirky today; they're outrageous!

I find them hunkered down in the living room, poring over the letter. I can tell by the lines on their face that this is serious business.

"What is it?" I ask, a little nervous for the answer.

Dad folds a letter and puts it back in the envelope. He takes Mom's hand. Mom nods as if agreeing with something he hasn't said out loud yet. She takes in a deep, deep breath.

"A woman has contacted us regarding your birthright," Dad says.

"Come here," Mom says, her voice breaking. "Sit. Next to me."

I sit. And gulp out the words, "Birth? Right?"

"You know we love you very much, don't you?" Mom asks.

I nod. "I love you, too." I can't help but think someone is dying.

"Many, many years ago," Mom pauses, like she's reading a fairy tale. "Many years ago on a beautiful morning, your dad and I heard the strangest thing. It was a baby crying. We opened the front door and saw a baby in a basket, wrapped in a pink blanket. There was an envelope." She stops and stares into space. Whatever it is she wants to tell me, isn't spilling out easily.

Dad fiddles with the sleeve on his flannel shirt. "An envelope, one similar to the envelope you found in the mail, was pinned to that baby's blanket. The handwriting matches. They're from the same person."

"What does this have to do with me?" I ask.

Mom draws me closer. "That baby was *you*. The note was addressed to us. It said: *This is the child of B. Rose Aurora, and there is no one who can care for her. Please raise this motherless child as if she were your own.*"

I blink and blink again. This is a dream. I must be dreaming. Wait. I *did* have a dream about somebody finding something on a doorstep recently. Now I remember. Mom and Dad were talking doggies and they found a puppy in a basket.

"I don't get it," I say nervously. "You lost me and a stranger found me and left me outside?"

Mom keeps pressing her fingers together and then waving them frantically in the air. "No, Bernie. Your dad and I were . . . jeepers, creepers, this is hard. You dad and I were getting up in years and still childless. The person who left you at our door asked us to be your parents."

"Hold up. You *are* my parents. What's going on? Is this a joke?" A few tears have started trickling down my cheek. I attack them with my fist.

Mom and Dad slowly tell me that what I've known to be true my entire life is a big, fat lie. They are not my biological parents! A baby arrived on their doorstep and that baby was me! They took me in and raised me as their own.

I pound a couch pillow. "Who are my parents? Are they still alive? How did I get here? Where did I come from?"

Mom pries open my fists and takes my hands in hers. "We wanted a baby more than anything, Bernie," she explains. "I believe you were sent from heaven. The angels saw that we were lonely. They gave us you."

I stand up. My stomach juices are boiling. "Did the angels tell you my real name?"

"No," Mom says.

"Do I have a birth certificate?"

"Not really," Dad says. "We know your real mother's name: B. Rose Aurora. We gave you her name, sort of. We didn't know what the B stood for so we named you Bernice."

"That's how I got stuck with Bernice Rose?"

Mom and Dad nod, like bobblehead dolls on the dashboard of a speeding car.

B. Rose Aurora. My real mother's name. I wonder what her first name is. Chances are it's not Bernice. I, Bernice Rose Baransky, ended up in Porchtown with a fill-in-the blank name and fill-in-the blank parents.

"Am I adopted?"

"Not really," Dad says again.

"Stop saying not really!" I yell. "I want to know who my parents are. Am I adopted or not?"

Dad gives in. "No. We never thought we needed to adopt you. You were already ours."

I can't speak. I've always understood my parents to be a little strange, but this is ridiculous. It's not right. It's not even legal!

I spit out, "Why now? Why are you telling me this now?"

Dad holds up the opened envelope. A letter falls out, and he quickly scoops it up. "Someone has been asking questions about you," he says. "It's the same person who left you at our door."

"Questions? What questions?" I pace around the living room like a caged animal.

"Like, are you happy with us? Like, have we told you what we've just told you?"

"Why would they care?" I ask. "He or she ditched me."

"It is worrisome, sweetie," Mom says. "And I kid you not. They can't have you back."

I rub my shaky thighs. I want to rub out this ridiculous news and have things return to normal.

"Wait," I say to my parents, taking it all in. "They want me back?"

The Maiden's Lost Mojo

For the last twenty-four hours, I have searched and searched for the letter. There must be more to it than what my parents are telling me. I've torn apart bedrooms, bathrooms, and closets. It's not hiding in the pantry, cutting a rug in the garage, or dangling from a hook in Dad's tackle box. It's nowhere.

Mom and Dad have gone into reassurance overdrive, telling me I have nothing to worry about. They tell me to stop searching for the letter because it means nothing. I want to believe them. But I'd still like to read it since the person who wrote it asked about me. I want to tell that person that I, Bernice Rose Baransky, am basically happy. I like my life. And even though I've wished for a couple of things to change this summer, a change in parents was not one of them!

I need to get to the park. I may be a little lost as to my birthright, but I know one thing for sure. I. Am. A. Skater.

Once outside, I see it's starting to drizzle. Rain is a skater's worst enemy. We hate rain. It messes with our trucks, and a slick surface is a nightmare. I don't care about any of that. I ride to the park.

As soon as I get inside the gate, Wyatt sees me. My heart thumps out of my chest and lands somewhere south of my knees.

"Yo, Bernie!" he calls, cruising over.

"You can call me Dude if you want," I say.

Wyatt shrugs. "Ready to channel your inner terminator and hit the half?"

"I've got no mojo today."

Wyatt doesn't push, which I appreciate. I warm up on the small ramps, and watch as Wyatt ollies up and slides down ledges and ramps, rips across the volcano, attacks the hubbas, jumps the steps, and works his latest bit of awesomeness—the Smith grind. I fail on my last trick—an attempt at a tailslide and decide to practice kick flips and my 50-50 instead. Nine out of ten times my butt gets a nice introduction to the ground. Nothing is going right. I can't even blame the rain because it stopped fifteen minutes ago and the sun is out.

Wyatt zips around the obstacles, but slows down when he comes near me. As he rides past, he tugs my hair, light as a summer breeze. It tickles. My pulse does a few ollies of its own. My knees tremble like they do on Dad's boat when we bump around in rough water. My lips have taken a vacation.

But my mojo? My mojo is back!

"Up for a little rock and roll?" Wyatt calls.

"Sure," I tell him.

When we're at the top of the half-pipe, Wyatt stands behind me. "Go for it," he says.

I give him a quick wave, push off, and fly down the vert. My run starts out clean, but toward the bottom something's terribly wrong! It's not my knees that are knocking, it's my board. Oh, no! I've got the wobbles. My trucks are loose! With all the distractions I've had, I didn't check the bolts, bearings, and screws like I usually do. And my constant mess-ups earlier must've loosened everything.

It's pretty clear I can't make it up the other side. No rock and roll for me. At this rate, I'll never master it. At the bottom of the ramp, I grab my board and shuffle off the half-pipe. I'm the biggest skater dog to ever poop out on the pipe.

Wyatt comes over and stands close to me. Uncomfortably close. "Speed wobbles," he says. "It happens."

Wyatt understands. I could hug him, but I need at least twenty more social graces lessons before moving up to impulsive hug.

"I can show you an easier trick, if you want," Wyatt offers.

"No! I'll get this. I swear. I'll prove it."

"You've got nothing to prove to me, Bernie." Wyatt plants a foot on his board. "Listen, I've gotta run. I've got an extra baseball practice at five."

I want to keep Wyatt here for a little longer, so I muster up more questions like Odelia has taught me. "Where's your practice?" I ask. "At the south end field? Or the north one? How long are your practices? Are you coming back to skate afterwards?" Five questions. Fired off like a robotic TV reporter grilling a sports star after a game.

Wyatt answers, "South. Until dark. See ya."

Ugh. I stink at this conversation stuff.

I move to a spot on the bleachers and inhale what's left in my water bottle. A father and son enter the park. The dad is carrying a mini skateboard for his boy who's probably no older than five or six. The kid is talking fast—so fast that his poor dad can't get a word in. And he's running around acting as if he's trying to jump invisible hurdles. Between the speed of his language and the speed of his legs, the boy screams attention deficit. How is this dad ever going to get this kid to settle down enough to teach him how to skateboard?

"Denny," the dad says, "you've been begging me for weeks to come to the park. We're here, so let me show you how to ride. We'll take it step by step. Hop on. I've got you."

Denny steps on. Denny steps off. The dad picks him up and puts him on. Denny jumps off, laughing. More hurdle hopping again. When Denny finally sticks to the board, he thinks he's an expert. He pushes off too hard, and does a faceplant into the concrete. "I'm bad at this," he whines. He stamps his feet and has a full-out temper tantrum.

Dad waits for the outburst to be over. "Let's try riding together. Get on. I'll push off and step on the back."

Eventually, the dad teaches Denny how to ride on his own. All it took was patience. Denny will be tackling the mini ramp by the end of the day.

I bet I could do what Denny's dad did. I could teach the Smile Academy kids how to skate! They need to let out their bottled-up energy and get some exercise. They need to get outside and enjoy what's left of the summer. And *I* need to have something to keep my mind off everything that's going on!

Dressed for the Part
or Partly Dressed

It's Tuesday, Prince and Princess Day at Smile Academy. I'm in my room, staring at the ceiling fan, trying to get myself in a partying mood. I push my comfy sheets to my feet, lean over the side of my bed, and search for a shoebox. I've been putting random junk in that box since I was two—junk I didn't have the heart to throw out. On top, there's the red ribbon I got last February. I entered a poster contest about bike safety and won. DON'T BE LIKE MIKE, it said. WEAR A HELMET WHEN RIDING YOUR BIKE. I drew a boy upside on his bike, seconds away from crashing. The poster still hangs in the Porchtown Police Station.

There are lots of photos of me and Roxanne from third grade, the year I got a camera for my birthday. There's a bouncy ball, a charm bracelet from Aunt Winnie that I never wore, a used-up iTunes gift card, four glass beads, a star-shaped magnet that says YOU CAN'T KEEP ME FROM SHINING, and a Valentine's Day card I was too embarrassed to give to Max Murphy, this second-grader who never got one from anybody. There's a five-by-seven picture of me dressed as Cinderella, taken by a professional photographer. I remember that day like it was yesterday. I was miserable because the photographer wouldn't let me wear my battery-operated, light-up tiara because of the glare it caused.

I push all that junk aside and find what I want—my princess stash from years ago. There's my favorite plastic golden tiara with plastic "jewels," a candy "ruby" ring with a matching chewable necklace, a pair of anklets with frilly lace tops, and a magic wand. Looking at my old princess accessories puts me in a better mood.

"That's a great collection." Odelia's popped into my room and is sitting on the edge of my bed.

"You're dressed for the party already? You look beautiful."

Odelia's wearing the same fuchsia gown she wore when she showed up on my street in a pink convertible. Gold earrings dangle from her dainty earlobes. They match the gold-and-pink topaz necklace around her neck. These are new. I've never seen them before. Her hair is up and the tiara that's perched on top catches the morning sunlight and makes random streaks on my dark green walls. I had gotten used to Odelia dressing like a regular kid, so I'm kind of stunned by her beauty. I almost forgot she was a princess. I mean, I almost forgot she *thought* she was a princess.

"I'm looking forward to today," Odelia says. "Is the jewelry too much? I never get to wear it anymore, so I thought . . . Oh, I don't know what to think. Should I take it off?"

I never thought I'd see a day when Odelia was unsure of herself. For once, it's my turn to reassure her. "Don't take off the jewelry," I say. "With or without your accessories, you are a perfect princess. Deal with it."

"Thank you," she says. "And you are far more than rather plain."

I squeak out, "Thank you," and am secretly proud of myself for remembering my manners.

"To be honest," Odelia begins, "Serena has mentioned more than once that I have ogre-size shoulders and—according to you—feet the size of a giant and the gluteus maximus of an Olympic gymnast. Also, I've been cursed with hair that when twisted into a bun invites a sparrow to nest. I am, as you say, a dork."

I giggle. "That's why that sparrow follows you everywhere?" I ask.

Odelia nods. "Dang, that bird is annoying!"

A smile creeps up on me. Odelia is less and less proper every day. "What's in the bag?"

"It is a gift for you. Please open it. I can't wait to hear what you think of it."

I lift up the end of the soft fabric bag and see a gown exactly like Odelia described the other day. It's the color of a rose—not a deep, dark-red rose, but a light rosy rose. I can't resist running my fingers over the soft material. The sash is white. It's gathered into an enormous bow in the back. The satin slippers match the sash and each one has a rosy bow. It is the best princess outfit I've ever seen!

"Do you like it?" Odelia asks.

"I do," I tell her. "But I'm finding it hard to be in a party mood."

Odelia puts on a scowl fit for a cranky old grandma. "If you don't come, the campers will be disappointed."

I can't argue with that. I touch the dress and it feels bouncy. I check under the skirt. "Can I ditch this netted stuff? It'll scratch me."

"I guess you can ditch the tulle slip. Put it on and see if it fits. My seamstress is extraordinary and I tried to explain what size you were, but she's not a magician. If it's not accommodating, we can make alterations."

"Accommodating? Alterations?" I ask. "Stop making everything sound like a royal proclamation!"

"If it doesn't fit, we'll fix it," Odelia answers abruptly.

Odelia shoves me out of bed. In five minutes, I'm transformed. The slippers are surprisingly cushiony, but the gown is droopy, a problem that, Odelia reminds me, can be solved by adding the scratchy slip.

"Pass?" I ask.

"Pass," Odelia answers. "Don't you feel awesome?"

"Awkward," I tell her. "As in not awesome."

"The Smile Academy kids adore you, and they'll brighten your day. They always do, don't they?"

"Especially Nellie," I say. "But after today, I won't see her anymore."

Odelia raises that left eyebrow. "Are you going to tell me what is truly making you sad? Aside from Nellie?"

I plop on my bed and the gown makes a swishy noise as it settles around me. "My parents aren't my parents."

"I don't understand," Odelia says.

"My real mother—the one who gave birth to me—didn't want to take care of me. She, or somebody who knew her, dumped me on our doorstep shortly after I was born and left George and Ellie Baransky to raise me."

Odelia drops her mouth wide-open. She's frozen.

"Not a good look for a princess," I say. "That bird may decide to perch in there instead of in your hair."

"You found this out recently?"

I nod.

"How terrible!" Odelia shouts. "And yet, it's another thing we have in common besides our matching middle names. I've also been raised by someone other than my parents."

"I would have had a different life if my real parents raised me," I say.

"And I would've had a different one if my parents had lived. But, Bernice, things have turned out fine for us."

"My parents had a choice. Yours didn't. Can you tell me how they died?"

While I wait for her to answer, I slip on the candy "ruby" ring from my shoebox and take a lick. It's disgusting, but I keep licking it anyway.

Odelia swallows hard. "I was one and a half when my mother and father passed away. Serena says that my mother died of a 'womanly problem.' She's never told me the details. My father died of a broken heart, shortly thereafter. I should know more, but I don't."

"I should know more, too," I say. "All I know is that my middle name, Rose, is also my mother's middle name. Other than that, I have no idea who I am."

"Whoever you are, Bernice Rose," Odelia says, taking both my hands in hers, carefully avoiding my sticky ring, "I, Odelia Rose, think you're amazing. Your plight has made me realize that I don't want to live in the dark about my mother and father's death any longer. I have to find out what Serena has never told me."

"I feel like I'm still in the dark. It'd be nice if both of us got some answers. No one dumps me on a doorstep and gets away with it."

Odelia and I walk to Smile Academy. Truth is, I'm walking; Odelia's dodging the sparrow that's flitting around her like an annoying mosquito. She's humming a catchy tune, and I can't help but hum along with her. She may be a weirdo at times, but she's become my weirdo friend. I'm glad she moved in across the street this summer.

The entire academy has storybook kingdom decorations. In the large playroom, castle turrets have been painted on long pieces of paper and hang from the blackboards. A three-foot stuffed dragon sits in the corner next to a greenish-blue rug that's supposed to be the moat. Plastic fish "swim" on the moat. Miss Robyn sure has been busy!

Miss Robyn runs over to us. "You two are absolutely gorgeous! What authentic-looking princess gowns! They make this old bridesmaid dress of mine appear ordinary."

"Your dress is very pretty," Odelia assures her.

"Thank you, Odelia. By the way, girls, we have a new volunteer. Roxanne will be here today and perhaps a few other days going forward. Roxanne, come over here!"

Roxanne is volunteering?

"Bernie!" Roxanne shouts, skipping over. "I got the idea from you. I had to stop moping around and get out of my house. The kids here let me do their hair!"

"Maybe your mom will hold up on the New York trips now," I tell Roxanne.

"Duh. That's the plan," Roxanne says.

I'm glad to see her. If she's here on Mondays and Wednesdays, and I'm here Tuesdays and Thursdays, we can get together on Fridays and share our Smile Academy stories. I may even let her in on the unbelievable things in my life, like Bernice Baransky's friend Odelia has been dishing out social graces lessons. And, Bernice Baransky is not the daughter of Mr. and Mrs. Baransky. News at eleven.

Roxanne twirls me around. "Holy Sister Mary and Joseph! What a dress! I couldn't find a thing to wear except this old Halloween costume, but yours is fabulous!" Then she leads me over to a chair. "Sit down. Let's get you some princess hair, like this princess." She points to Odelia and I quickly introduce them.

Roxanne squeezes gel into my hair, flips what she can to the top of my head, adds thirty bobby pins to capture the escapees, and seals the deal with her mega hairspray. When she's finished, my hair is completely pulled up and back. Curly pieces dangle in front of my ears. The girl campers ooh and aah over my 'do and each one squeals, hoping they're Roxy, Super Stylist to the Star's next victim.

Prince Robbie, Timothy, Joe, Sammy, Angelo, and the rest of the boys fight the stuffed dragon with swords made from soft foam. Princess Claire is running around screaming, "Save me! Save me!" and the other princesses are copying her. It's mayhem. And mayhem is exactly what I need today.

While the kids have a tea party, I pull Miss Robyn into her office and explain my idea to teach them skating. "I could stay past noon, and start with skateboarding lessons on the camp's parking lot. I can teach them to ride and stop, and maybe show them a couple of basic tricks. They'd love it."

"Where would they get skateboards?" Miss Robyn asks. "And safety equipment? It would have to be highly supervised. The moms and dads will have to supply the equipment because there's not enough money in our account to fund this. And what if they think that skateboarding is not an appropriate activity? I don't want to be pessimistic, but we're asking a lot of the parents here. They may not go for it."

"Skateboarding is not a crime," I say. "It's good exercise. And I bet Porchtown Sports would donate some used boards, helmets, wrist guards, elbow, and knee pads."

Miss Robyn likes my idea more and more. We draft a letter and a permission slip to send home to the parents.

"I'll send the information home and ask for the signed slips by Thursday. When you come in that day, we can see who's responded."

"Thanks, Miss Robyn. I'll keep my fingers crossed. I hope we can do this. You can learn to skate with them."

Miss Robyn rolls her eyes, chuckles, and shoos me back to the playroom.

I stick around for the rest of the party. Odelia and Roxanne are bonding over hairstyles, and I butt in to tell them about my plan.

"That sounds like fun," Odelia says. "I can help."

"Can I help?" Roxanne asks.

"You can't skate," I remind her.

"Maybe you can teach me."

"Teach you to skate? On a board? I'd like to see you try!"

Roxanne sticks her tongue out at me. "So, will you ask Wyatt to help out with the kids?"

"Maybe. He's a good teacher."

"He'd do it," Roxanne says. "He likes you."

"Since when did you get so smart about boys?"

"Since Kyle, this kid in my Sunday youth group, started paying lots of attention to me," Roxanne answers. "I'm blessed!"

Leave it to Roxanne to pray for attention from a boy and get results. I promise her I'll get up the guts to ask for Wyatt's help. There's a part of me that wants to do this. Then there's this other part that's afraid to learn Wyatt Anderson's true colors. What if he thinks it's not cool to hang out so much with the campers? If I have to choose between him and them, I don't know what I'd do.

The Sporty Dorkling

By Thursday the kids who are allowed to participate have sent in their permission slips. The kids who will not be skating are going for a walk with another counselor. Jessica is not happy about walking, because she wants to be with her friend Elizabeth, who will be learning to skate. Jessica's parents didn't sign her up for skateboarding lessons because she's leaving for vacation next week and won't be back in time to finish the lessons. I told Jess she can be our official water bottle carrier. I've never seen someone so happy about water.

While the kids are eating lunch, Odelia, Roxanne, and I meet in the parking lot. We line up orange cones in a big square and use sidewalk chalk to write: SKATER SAFETY AREA. We're starting here, and then moving to the skate park, if the kids cooperate. Miss Robyn will come along to supervise and the other counselors will stay with the non-skaters.

"Hey, Bernie," Roxanne shouts. "What happened to the skater grunge look? I thought for sure you'd change into your usual raggedy tee and those awful cut-offs."

"My mom uses those for cleaning rags now," I tell her.

"About time!" Roxanne says. "I'm loving those orange shorts. I don't think they match your hot pink shoes, but you have on pink. PINK! Wow!"

"They're pink *sneakers*," I say. "Stop obsessing and get over here so I can teach you how to ride that clunker of a board you're holding. The kids will be out here soon. If you want to help, you've got to be able to skate, at least."

Roxanne jogs over. She's decked out in a white-and-turquoise helmet, knee, elbow, and wrist guards. She's wearing gloves, too, probably because they go with everything else.

After five minutes, I realize two things: One, Roxanne is not a fast learner, and two, she's about as coordinated as an elephant on a snowboard.

"The last time you had your left foot forward; now, it's your right!" I yell. "C'mon, Roxanne, get with it. Decide!"

Roxanne is a wreck. "They both feel the same. I have no balance. It doesn't matter which foot is in front."

"Just pick one. Which is more comfortable?"

"Neither!" Roxanne shouts. "Don't let go of me, Bernie. BERNIE! Hold my hand!"

"I am. Stop being a wuss. Try it on your own, will you? Please?"

In a moment of bravery, Roxanne yanks herself away from me and shoves off, riding straight to the edge of the parking lot. When she hits the dirt, the board stops, and she does a faceplant onto the ground.

"That was lame, Roxanne. Seriously."

"I hate skateboarding," she says. She throws her board to the side, and storms inside.

I jump on my board and catch up to Odelia, who's riding my old longboard, looking quite comfy on it. She's weaving in and out of the cones as effortlessly as a surfer on a wave. "Roxanne is hopeless," I tell her. "She can't go three feet. It's pitiful."

"I heard," Odelia answers. Then she swerves in front of me and cuts me off. I have to stomp my foot down to keep from slamming into her! "When you teach, an ugly part of your personality rears its ugly head."

"What's on your mind, Odelia?"

"Why, another lesson, of course." From her backpack, she pulls out her trusty guide. I grab it, and read it in a hurry:

"ODELIA'S GUIDE TO THE SOCIAL GRACES

LESSON 11: DON'T BE A SPORTY DORK

OBJECTIVE: Bernice will discover how being a good teacher begins with being a good sport. (Note: Bernice's sportsmanship reminds me of the huntsman who lost his patience with the sport because the deer did not shoot itself.)"

I toss the notebook back to Odelia. "What do you expect me to do?"

"Remember when you showed Robbie and Claire how to build a tower? You had to be really sweet and patient."

"I lost all my patience today. I'm such a loser," I say. Some days I feel like the whole world is out to get me.

"You're not a loser," Odelia says. "Look at how far you've come with Wyatt. Treat everyone like you treat him. Be nice. You'll reap the rewards of your efforts. Just as I have reaped the rewards of being your social graces teacher."

"What reward did you get?" I ask.

"Haven't you figured it out, Bernice? I have fulfilled my responsibility to Serena. She asked that we become friends, and we have!" Odelia looks at me with questioning eyes, and I give her a quick shoulder nudge to reassure her.

"Good friends," I say. No doubt about it. Odelia is my good friend. I truly like her. And look how she's changed! No more princess gowns! She's wearing a purple-and-maroon skirt that is slightly above her knees, a gauzy peasant shirt, and a crocheted vest with a sun and a moon on the front. The Bohemian vibe suits her. I wonder if her personal seamstress made these or if Serena bought them. Which reminds me, "Hey, Odelia, did you push Serena for info on your parents' deaths. Did you find out anything?"

Odelia stops. "How considerate of you to ask!" She pops up her skateboard to her hand and I do the same. We walk to the door where the kids are lining up, ready to join us. "Serena doesn't give out information easily." Odelia picks at her nail polish and a bit chips off. "I prodded and pried and discovered that my father lived only one week following the death of my mother. Many years ago, I was told he died of a broken heart. I've assumed he was so saddened by my mother's death that he couldn't go on. But I was wrong. My father died of a heart that *was* broken. Serena tells me that he had severe pains in his chest and his heart simply stopped."

"A heart attack?"

"Yes." Odelia continues. "And there's more. I know that my mother died; however, and this has been a family secret that Serena has kept, she died in *childbirth*."

"That is so sad," I say. "And the baby?"

"There is no baby." Odelia sniffs. "I don't have a sibling."

I wrap my arms around Odelia. Both our families are super secret-keepers.

"We need to have some fun," I tell Odelia. "There are campers here who have to learn to skate."

Odelia raises her left eyebrow.

"I promise not to be a sporty dork," I tell her.

26

MADE OF AWESOME!

The Three Little Bigs

When the kids come out after lunch, I recognize Robbie, Elizabeth, Claire, Timothy, Angelo, Joe, and Sammy, but others I know aren't here. And Nellie is missing, which makes me very sad. Some of the parents have showed up to watch, which I appreciate because at least two campers outweigh me by ten pounds.

Miss Robyn joins us. She has on her safety gear and a sweet-looking skateboard sits at her feet. She touches a toe to the nose, pushes it forward and rocks it back. I get the feeling she's not about to stand on it anytime soon.

"I love your board!" I tell her. "The graphics are awesome."

This may have been a mistake. The kids break out in a "Made of awesome! Made of awesome!" cheer. It takes Miss Robyn a few minutes to calm them down and get them back on track.

Odelia takes the lesser coordinated kids to the safety zone. She politely asks Roxanne for her help, and Roxanne skips behind her like an obedient toddler. Odelia shows them how to step on and off without the board sliding away. Some kids get comfortable enough to stand and roll. Roxanne gives it another go, too. Odelia's definitely a better teacher than I am. I wouldn't be surprised if she pulled out a new notebook with the words: ODELIA'S GUIDE TO BEGINNING BOARDING on it.

Timothy is the first camper-slash-skater that I take aside. Since he's Smile Academy's best hopscotcher, I'm hoping he's not afraid of hopping on a skateboard. I ask him if he's ever been skating, and he shouts, "No! No! No!" He presses both fists into his sides by his ribs. A second later, he jumps on his slightly worn board, and latches on to my shoulder with a death grip. He bounces up and down on it like it's a trampoline and falls on his butt. I wait for him to cry, but he doesn't. He laughs and holds out his hands so I can help him up. He hops on the board with both feet and clings to me.

Before he becomes a human jumping bean again, I tell him calmly, "Timothy, see the wheels? You *roll* on a skateboard."

I attempt to peel his clenched fingers from my collar bone and take the board away from him to demonstrate, and this time he *does* have a meltdown. He stomps one foot, then the other. He pouts the biggest pout I've ever seen. I take a deep breath and promise myself I will not say anything I'll regret. I have to stay under control. It's not easy! Lucky for me, Timothy's dad, who has been watching us from the doorway, comes to my rescue. He says the right words to put his son in a happy place.

After a half-hour, there's progress. I do what Odelia has suggested and take things step-by-step. I also compliment him. Listening to myself say, "Yes, you can do it!" and "Please try again!" I sound like a cross between Odelia and my sixth-grade art teacher, the super spunky lady who occasionally raved about my drawings. Timothy eventually learns to skate six feet before the jumping begins again. I'm proud of him. His enthusiasm rocks!

Camper-slash-skater number two is a Nellie look-alike in size and shape. Unlike Nellie, who has an electric personality, Elizabeth is quiet. She slinks over to me like a scared snake. I've only seen Elizabeth at camp once or twice. She's *always* quiet.

"Elizabeth, are you sure you want to try this?" I ask.

She shrugs.

I touch her brand-new skateboard. It's a longboard, not actually made for doing tricks. That's fine, but how am I going to teach her to ride it if she won't talk to me?

"It's a great skateboard," I say to Elizabeth.

She nods.

"And I like those flower stickers on your helmet."

She nods again. I find Elizabeth's mom leaning against the fence. She's smiling. This gives me hope that I'm not messing up. I think back to how that dad taught his young son. They rode together. I stand on the board and ask Elizabeth if she wants to sit on it in front of me with her feet scrunched up to her chest and her hands holding on behind. Elizabeth doesn't seem confident enough to stand. Plus, since she's short, soft, and round, and I'm the opposite; our center of gravity will be off.

"Ready, set, go?" I ask.

"Go," she whispers.

I push off, take it easy, and gently rock the board, slowly making wide turns around the other campers. We cruise past Odelia who is showing Robbie, Claire, and Joe how to step on the back part of the board so it lifts and you can grab it. They're having a blast. We ride around Miss Robyn who is teaching the rest of the group how *not* to use the board as a hat, a bat, or a push toy. I'm so proud of everyone, I could burst.

Next, I weave around the cones, and Elizabeth wails.

Uh, oh! I got carried away. I've scared her. I slam down my foot and stop.

"Faster!" Elizabeth yells.

Oh! She *likes* it! Elizabeth may not say much, but she's clearly in love with skateboarding.

Because everybody is being cooperative, Miss Robyn suggests we take the skaters to the park. I'm up for anything.

When we get there, I see Wyatt. He waves. I wave back. I hate to admit it, but I'm officially a waver now.

He asks, "What's up? You here to practice the rock and roll?"

"I . . . um . . . I'm kind of busy."

Wyatt checks out the kids. "Busy?"

"Volunteering," I answer, and wait for the disgust to show up on his face.

"What?"

"I volunteer at that camp I told you about—Smile Academy. I do it twice a week. We're here because I'm showing them how to skate."

Wyatt looks from camper to camper. "Decent," he says. "You want help?"

"Definitely! Can you check out everybody's boards to make sure the decks are free of cracks, the grip tape is sealed on tight, the bearings are okay, and the trucks and wheels aren't loose?"

"No speed wobbles," he says, winking.

I blush. "Just wobbly campers."

For the next hour, we're like a sports team running drills. After Wyatt's finished with the boards, he helps Tony, or Hawk, as Wyatt has nicknamed him, after Tony Hawk, pro skater. Hawk knows how to skate a little, so Wyatt teaches him how to ride up the small ramp, do a kick turn, and ride down again. Wyatt's balancing on the coping to keep Hawk from going too far and flying off the platform. He gives Hawk a push when he gets close to the top so he gets turned around and can go back down with the right foot forward. It takes a lot of effort. There's a lot of loud grunting, whooping, and hollering, but neither Wyatt nor Hawk say words that will get them kicked out of the park.

When it's time to go, the campers look sweaty and exhausted, but their faces are bright. I bet Miss Robyn will have a room full of happy nappers by five o'clock.

Seeing how much they like skateboarding gives me an idea—an off-the-wall idea. What if they got to be in the skate-off? Like in a special division or something. As part of their own Mighty Munchkin Skate Team. How cool would that be!

"Hey, Miss Robyn," I yell, as we're leaving. "Did you see that sign on the gate about the Lawrence County Skate-Off?"

Mirror, Mirror

The whole way home I'm pretty happy with myself. Miss Robyn liked the idea of getting the campers involved in a community event. She's planning to make some calls to see if the kids can be included. "It'll heighten awareness of the abilities of Down syndrome children," she told me.

When I open our front door, the first thing I see is Mom and Dad. Dad's John Lennon–inspired bifocals have slid to the tip of his nose. He's fallen asleep on the recliner, and I'm guessing he never got through the magazine that's on his lap—the one with the huge trout on its cover. Mom gives him a peck on the cheek and cozies up with her crafts on the couch. Her face is bright and alive, but her hair is bluish gray. For a second, I see a portrait of my parents that catches me off guard. They are old! I didn't come into their lives until they were in their fifties. And I showed up because my mother, B. Rose Aurora, couldn't care for me. Is B. Rose crazy? Maybe she's been in a loony bin for the last twelve years. Maybe she's a spy. Maybe it's simpler than any of the above reasons. Maybe she didn't want to be my mom. Or, maybe she's dead.

I still worry a bit about who's checking up on me. That person doesn't need to. I'm fine. George and Ellie Baransky have been great parents. I have lived in a happily-ever-after household. I want to let the birthright thing go, but it's hard.

"Something bugging you, Bern?" Dad asks, stretching.

"Can you tell me exactly what's in that letter—my birthright letter? Please? Where is that letter?"

"Oh, we shoved it away somewhere," Mom answers. "Bernie, don't have a cow about—"

"Things you can't change," Dad says, finishing her sentence, as usual.

"The person who wrote that letter wanted us to tell you things. We did. And they wanted reassurance that you were doing well. You are. Everything's cool-o-roonie."

"That's it?"

"That's it, sweetie," Mom says. "Leave it be."

I don't push, which Mom and Dad appreciate. I feel like the situation is hopeless and not hopeless. I'm curious, but not that curious. I have a lot of other things to think about, and I'm grateful for that.

In my room, I turn my attention to the skate-off. I've got to get to the park more often to master the rock and roll. I'll have it down soon if I can get some practice in. On paper, I write down some tricks I want the campers to learn, if they can compete. Then I give Roxanne a call to fill her in.

"And I'm also sorry for having zero patience when you were trying to skateboard," I say. "Odelia pointed that out to me."

"I forgive you," Roxanne says. "Odelia's super nice. But even she can't teach me to skate. I am not a skater. I won't be any help getting the kids in shape for the skate-off."

"Why don't you fix their hair before the competition?"

Roxanne's not answering.

"Roxanne?"

"Don't they have to wear helmets?" she asks. I can feel her brain cells zapping a mile a minute through the phone.

"Yeah, but . . ."

"I could give the girls matching ponytails. Ooh, and add glitter to the ends or . . . let's see, what about wash-out dye? What to do for the boys? I'll come up with something. Maybe face paint? Or temporary tattoos. And make-up. Everyone in a show needs make-up. Even you, Bernie!"

"No, I don't," I say. "So, you'll work your magic on the kids?"

Roxanne giggles. "Roxy, Super Stylist to *Your* Stars, at your service."

The next day at noon, I meet Odelia in the street and together we skate to Smile Academy. It's not our day to be there, but we're both looking forward to an afternoon skate session with the kids. Odelia's thrilled that she and the campers may get to be a part of the skate-off. When we roll around to the parking lot, Miss Robyn calls us over for a quick meeting.

"I phoned the president of the council last night," she says, "to make a plea to allow the campers to perform at the skate-off. I didn't want to waste any time. He said he'll have to clear it with the judges and the committee, but he doesn't see a problem. He thinks it's an excellent addition to the program."

Odelia and I both shout, "Yay!"

"It's up to you," Miss Robyn says. "You have two short weeks to turn our campers into skateboarders." Miss Robyn winks. "Our goal is to have them shine in their own right, nothing more. The council assured me that each camper will get a big blue ribbon for their participation."

This makes me feel better. I'd hate it if they didn't win something.

When the kids file out, we stay in the parking lot to review how to stop and go and how to skate safely without running into each other. It's like starting from scratch. No one seems to remember anything! Elizabeth, who yesterday finally got up the nerve to stand on her board herself, has forgotten how. Robbie and Angelo are being stubborn. They've decided to play Follow-the-Leader. Timothy wants to see how many jumping jacks he can complete in a minute. And Claire and her friends are stretched out on the ground, guessing which clouds look like farm animals.

I've had it. "Hey, don't you want to be skaters?" I shout. "I'm not doing this for my health."

The kids stop what they're doing. They don't get what I mean.

"You need to practice! Practice, practice, practice!" I say, waving my hands wildly, and then jamming them on my hips. I'm my mother on a day when she's yelling at her supplies. Or at me. "You can't give up now! Get your skateboards!" I don't care if I'm a sporty dork. I have to get through to the campers.

About half of the group starts skating. The others ignore me, and Miss Robyn says to leave them be. I teach Claire how to roll and stop, and kick the board into her hand. But Claire's glasses keep getting sweaty and sliding down her nose and everything's off by a couple of inches. I attempt to show Joe how to turn, but his favorite thing to do today is hug me, so I'm getting nowhere. Sammy's being cooperative, and he's discovered how fun it is to skate up my old, homemade mini ramp that Dad dropped off earlier. I need to stay downwind of Sammy because Sammy needs to discover something else—how not to fart in public.

We never make it to the skate park. Odelia is quiet on the ride home. I get the feeling I'm in for a lesson, although I can't imagine what it would be. When we get near my house, she pulls out the guide, and I read it out loud:

"ODELIA'S GUIDE TO THE SOCIAL GRACES

LESSON 12: BE A MIRROR TO THYSELF

OBJECTIVE: Bernice will practice . . ."

I slam the book shut. "I have been practicing! I've been practicing lessons one through eleven; I've been practicing with the Smile Academy kids; I've been practicing forever! My brain and body need a vacation."

"Finish reading, Bernice."

I open the notebook and say in a flat voice:

"LESSON 12: BE A MIRROR TO THYSELF

OBJECTIVE: Bernice will practice understanding others.
(Note to self: Bernice has the empathy
of a shepherd who can't figure out why the sheep run when
the farmer shows up with the clippers.)"

I roll my eyes. I'm lessoned out.

"Think about what causes people to act the way they do," Odelia says in her teacher voice.

By now, I'm sitting on my front porch, and Odelia is pacing up and down the sidewalk. I feel like I'm watching a sad documentary on my life.

"For example," Odelia continues, "Maybe Elizabeth didn't forget what she learned; maybe she got scared. And Robbie and Angelo weren't being stubborn; they were bored. Follow-the-Leader was more interesting. Also, you assumed that Timothy didn't want to practice because he was doing jumping jacks. To him, skating is like jumping and he *was* practicing. As for Claire, she's a dreamer. Remember what it's like to sit and dream, Bernice?"

Tiny tears are forming in the corners of my eyes. I quickly pinch my tear ducts and make them disappear. Odelia didn't see them, right?

"Walk in another person's shoes, Bernice," Odelia says. She clicks her heels together like Dorothy in the *Wizard of Oz*.

Those heels are getting blurry. I turn and do a couple of fake sneezes, so Odelia doesn't catch me being all emotional. Skaters don't get emotional. When I look up, she's gone.

I stay on my front steps for a half-hour. For the first time, three things are crystal clear: One, Odelia is far smarter than any thirteen-year-old I've ever met. Two, Roxanne is right. Odelia's nice. Tough, but nice. And three, there's a chance that by the time I get to middle school, the rough edges Odelia saw in me at the beginning of the summer will be as smooth as a newly sanded ramp. I, Bernice Baransky, will go to middle school with a few social skills. Skills that will help me fit into a scary new school with scary people who aren't like me. Skills that will help me understand them. I sniffle because, well, that last thought deserves a sniffle.

Roxanne, Roxanne, Let Down Their Hair

We've been practicing almost every day, and the days fly by. In the Smile Academy parking lot and at the park, the kids have really stepped up. They've been tackling their tricks and perfecting them. It's like they've instantly discovered how cool it is to skate with each other. There's never a harsh word or a bad remark from one kid to the next. They're always smiling, even when they mess up. And I'm smiling a lot more, too. The Lawrence County Skate-Off is tomorrow, and I think we're ready.

Today Robbie, Joe, and Tony, who's officially Hawk, are watching Wyatt as he demonstrates how to ollie up small ledges. Their attention is glued on Wyatt's every word. If we can get through the next couple of hours of board-flipping before anyone knocks out a front tooth, I'll be happy. I'll be happier than happy if I can land my rock and roll at the competition. Since I've been spending a lot of time with the campers, my practice time has been cut in half.

I see Roxanne's mom's car parked near the gate of the skate park. When I get a break, I skate over to see what's going on. The tailgate is up and the back is stocked with a ton of hair and beauty supplies.

"How'd you get your mom to do this?" I ask. I pick up a hair tie and sweep my sweaty strands into a very short ponytail. It sticks out the back like an arrow. Roxanne makes a face. I've obviously committed a terrible hair crime.

"Easy," she says. "I asked Miss Robyn to call her and explain how she needed me to make the kids look their best. My mom couldn't say no, or she would look bad."

Claire skates over and Roxanne begins to twist pieces of her hair. It ends up in a complicated braid that starts by her ears and goes into a bow-like arrangement at the base of Claire's neck. "It's not bad, right?" Roxanne says, stepping back and admiring her work.

I squat so I'm eye-to-eye with Claire and straighten her glasses. "You are prettier than the prettiest doll in the store," I tell her. Claire giggles, shoves her helmet over her fancy hair, and skates away.

"Don't you care that their helmets crush your 'dos?"

"Nah. It's just to make them feel special. I'll do something else for the skate-off. Maybe spray-on highlights. Don't worry. Everyone will look fantastic. Don't forget. I want to do your hair and make-up, too."

I don't want to be gelled, sprayed, highlighted, and made-up by Roxy, Super Stylist to the Stars, but I don't tell her that. "Maybe," I say. "You're good at this, you know."

"I know," Roxanne says smugly. "It's much better than trekking up to New York and reciting three lines to a TV producer. Sure wish my mom would stop scheduling those darn auditions."

"When we're in middle school, maybe you can make her happy by joining the drama club—"

Roxanne interrupts, "I don't want to be an actress."

"Let me finish! I was going to say, join the club as a make-up artist."

"Great idea!" Roxanne says. "And maybe you should try out for a team sport. With the way you're able to move those feet, it'd be a cinch to pick up soccer."

I've never been on a team, except in gym class. I'm not team sport material. It'd be scary to learn soccer or lacrosse from scratch. I'd join the skateboarding team, if there was one.

Elizabeth is tugging on Roxanne's arm, and Roxanne sits her down and begins putting her soft brown hair into pigtails. "Middle school will be fun," Roxanne says just to me. "And you know what? I'll see Kyle every day, not only on Sundays."

Roxanne goes on about Kyle this and Kyle that, and then she pries me for info on Wyatt. It's sweet of her to ask, but I don't have anything to confess. Wyatt's still a puzzle to me. And as scary as a team sport.

Before we return to Smile Academy, we give the kids a pep talk. But they don't listen. They're busy goofing around on their boards. Whatever. They are totally into skating, and smiling from ear-to-ear, and that's what matters. We try to keep them under control so they don't get hurt. It's like trying to keep a litter of kitties in one place. I'm kind of relieved when it's time to say good-bye.

"Why did I agree to be a camp counselor, again?" I ask Odelia, as we skate home.

"You have a big heart," Odelia answers.

"A Baransky heart," I say. "My mom and dad are always helping people—each other, the neighbors, people in Mom's clubs, clueless fishermen who come into Jersey Bait and Tackle. Guess I got my heart from them. Not from B. Rose Aurora."

Odelia leaps off her skateboard before bothering to make it come to a full stop. The board almost rolls into the street. "B. Rose Aurora?" Odelia asks.

"Yeah," I say. "My mother. My real mother. Remember, I told you her middle name was Rose. Her full name was B. Rose Aurora and—"

Odelia cuts me off, which surprises me to no end because Odelia never forgets her manners. "And your middle name is her middle name," she says.

"It's kind of common, isn't it? *You* have it." Odelia's paler than her creamy pale shirt. "What wrong?"

Odelia paces up the sidewalk and down. "B? Rose? Aurora?"

"You heard me."

"Did you ever find out *who* left you on the doorstep?" Odelia asks, almost shouting. She's irritated with me. I have no idea why.

"No. It's in the letter they won't let me see. Why?"

"I must go," Odelia says in a hurry. "Serena is . . . Serena has . . . I've got to see Serena!"

With that, Odelia turns on the rocket boosters and boosts herself far ahead of me. This is so confusing. And extremely weird. Even for Odelia.

At dinner, Mom dishes out spaghetti and clams. It has to be one of the grossest meals on the planet. Globs of clams swim in a blood-red sauce. It's disgusting.

"Delish dish," Dad says.

I push the pasta around and make a gagging sound. "Please tell me this isn't made from leftover bait."

Dad winks. He's kidding, right?

I weed out the chunks of gooey clams and fill my parents in on how everything is going with the skate-off.

"Be there or be square. That's what I'm telling everybody," Mom says. She's told every crafter, knitter, baker, and candlestick maker in town.

"You've caught 'em hook, line, and sinker, hon," Dad adds, pulling her in for a smooch on the lips. At the dinner table! "There should be a dy-no-mite crowd," he adds. "Are you nervous, Bern?"

"I'm pretty sure I can do the tricks. It's not like I'll win a trophy or anything. I'm a little worried about the campers. I hope no one makes fun of them. And I'm kind of worried about Odelia. She flipped out at me today for no reason." I shove in a mouthful of spaghetti and try not to think about the clams as they slide down my throat. "Pass the parmesan cheese, please?"

Dad slides it across to me, but the container is empty.

"I'll get another one," I say.

"No," Mom says, jumping up. "Let me get it."

"I can reach it," I say, beating her to the highest shelf of the pantry. I inch the can toward the front. It falls into my hands. An envelope falls with it. A dingy yellow envelope.

I turn to Mom and Dad. Their look tells me what I've already figured out. It's the letter. With everything that's been going on, I almost forgot about it. Guess I wanted to believe everything's cool, that Mom and Dad were right. It didn't mean anything.

I stare at it. Mom doesn't grab it out of my hands, which I appreciate. Mom looks at Dad, and Dad says, "It's hunky-dory, hon. Let her see it."

I barge through the back door. In one swift move, I flip my board under my feet and roll at top speed away from my house. I race away to my home away from home—the skate park. The gate is locked. It's almost dark. I pick a spot under the street light, slide down the chain link fence, and open the envelope with shaky hands.

Dear Mr. and Mrs. Baransky,

I am the person who deposited the baby girl on your doorstep twelve years ago. I'd like to know, is she happy? Have you told her how she came to live with you?

Allow me to explain. Due to unfortunate circumstances, I found myself in the unnatural position of having to mother this baby. I learned of your longing to have a baby through a family connection I have in the United States. Believing I was failing miserably at the task, I made the trip to the US with the infant and left her in your capable hands. I did what I felt was a noble act, knowing that you would be loving parents to a baby who was not your own.

You must be wondering why I am contacting you after all this time. I have lived with immense guilt for my actions, and I have discovered that my actions have consequences far greater than I ever realized. I must begin to make amends.

For now, all that I ask of you is to let the child know how she came into your lives.

The signature! I recognize that name! Why did *she* dump me on the Baransky doorstep? I don't get it. I spring to my feet, but those feet are stuck to the ground. It's hard to unstick them and drag myself home. But I do. When I finally get to our front step, Mom and Dad are there, peering out the screen door.

"Bern," Dad says.

Mom pulls me inside. "We're sorry we didn't show you the letter sooner." She wraps me in a bear hug.

Dad puts his arms around both of us. "Don't worry, my cutie-patootie. You are a Baransky. Nothing else matters diddly. We're a Baransky sandwich."

They don't get how big this is! They don't understand that I know the person who wrote this letter. It's a name that leaves me with a zillion questions, like: Why was I tricked? What's been going on this summer? And who am I, really?

I am not in the mood to be a sandwich.

Hi Ho, Oh No, to the Skate-Off We Will Go

Come Saturday morning I get up and get ready for the Lawrence County Skate-Off. This is a special day for Smile Academy and the kids who go there. Despite what I've found in that letter, I have to finish what I started. Odelia is the only one who can help with the craziness I feel. I've tried to call her again and again, on her stupid house phone, of course. I've knocked on her door, and yelled her name in the middle of Station Street, but she doesn't answer. And her house has been darker than dark. It looks deserted.

I throw on a striped gray tee and black shorts. My goal is to blend in with the boys today, not stick out. I have no idea if any other girls have entered. Anyway, Wyatt said that participating in this kind of event is mostly about putting on a good show. Good thing, because I haven't actually mastered the rock and roll. I've been close. Today had better be the day it comes together.

At the park, council members are putting the finishing touches on a portable stage. A huge sign hangs over it:

PORCHTOWN WELCOMES
NO BOYS ALLOWED!
CONCERT WILL FOLLOW SKATE-OFF
PRIZE CEREMONY

No matter how I skate—if I land my tricks or do a faceplant in front of a hundred people—two things will happen: I'll hear my favorite band.

And most importantly, I'll get some answers from Odelia. If she shows up! The last thought does nothing to calm my nerves.

The bleachers are packed, and I scan the seats. Mom stands and calls out, "Be radical, Bernice!"

Dad chimes in, "To the max, Bern!"

They both shoot me thumbs-up signs. I pretend I'm not related to them. Wait. A. Minute. I'm *not* related to them.

The panel of judges consists of a random bunch. There's Elise Winters, the twenty-something surfer who is the secretary for Porchtown Parks and Rec; Jamie King, the old fart who shows up at the park to skate; Jeff Gregory, the publisher of *Faceplant* magazine; and Brandon Richards, a California semi-pro who recently got a sponsorship from Element, the skateboarding company.

I find the Mighty Munchkins Skate Team standing with Miss Robyn.

"Where's Odelia?" I ask Miss Robyn. And to myself I say: *She must be here. She's got to be here. I've got to talk to her soon!*

"She called and said she'll be late, but she's coming. Don't the kids look amazing? Roxanne has outdone herself!"

I look from face to happy face. The girls are wearing blue eye shadow and a little mascara. Roxanne has used face paint to paint a huge red star on each of their left cheeks and a smiley face on their right. Their hair is pulled into low ponytails and a bright blue streak runs through each one. The boys have a royal blue lightning bolt that runs from cheek to chin, and spiky hair, which will get smashed by their helmets, but that's okay. Miss Robyn made a special screened tee for each skater. A sequined girl or boy skateboarder is on the front along with the camper's name. The Smile Academy logo, a daisy with a big smile in the center, is on the back. Fifteen ready-to-go skaters stand proudly holding a balloon in one hand and their skateboards and gear in the other. They're an impressive bunch.

"Wyatt checked the equipment, and he checked the course," Miss Robyn says. "I think we can begin. This is exciting! Did you see Nellie and her family sitting over there?"

Nellie's dressed in a cheerleader outfit, holding her mom's hand. Even with the crowd noise I can hear her. "Three cheers for Bernice! Three cheers for Nellie! Nellie Frances O'Malley and Bernice Baransky are BFFs! We are made of awesome!"

The other kids call out, "Made of awesome! Made of awesome!"

They are the awesome ones. If I don't get moving, I'll lose it. Nobody here needs to see a weepy skateboarder. Skateboarders don't weep.

I line up the campers and seconds before we're supposed to begin, Wyatt sneaks up beside me, puts his hand in mine and says, "Let's bounce."

I'm stuck. My feet won't bounce, twitch, walk, run, roll, or anything else because, well, A. Boy. Is. Holding. My. Hand. A boy who has the ability to turn me into a rambling idiot when I try to have a real conversation. I'm so nervous, I yank my hand out of his.

"Sorry," Wyatt says, embarrassed. "It was Odelia's idea to hold hands as we cruised in."

"She's here?" I ask. "Odelia's here? Where?"

"I dunno. Somewhere." He doesn't try to hold my hand again, and my fingers suddenly feel lonely.

"I don't see her. I have to, to find her!" I stutter, scanning the bleachers, the park, the field. I look everywhere—everywhere except directly at Wyatt.

"She'll catch up. Don't worry," Wyatt says. "We've gotta bring the skaters in. They're making the intros." Wyatt cracks his knuckles. He reads my it's-okay-to-hold-my-hand expression, threads his fingers into mine, and leads me away. Another awkward moment is over and done.

Elizabeth is the first skater. She heads out on her longboard, carving in and around the ledges, steps, and quarter-pipe. If anyone would have told me she'd be able to do this weeks ago, I would have argued with them. But here she is, riding like she was born on a board. She thrills the crowd by coming within a foot of the top of the stairs before expertly swerving to the side. The crowd claps. Elizabeth steps off her board and bows. Then she runs to me and gives me a hug, and I can barely keep my eyes dry.

Next in line is Timothy. Timothy skates fifty feet, jumps off, jumps on, and skates a little farther. At the end, he does five jumping jacks, jumping on the board with his feet together, then straddling the board, one foot on each side and on the ground. I'm glad we figured out a good use for his jumping!

Hawk is up next. Wyatt's been helping him master the ramp, but Hawk isn't that great at it. He falls almost every time. Once, he almost broke his arm. We were convinced his parents would go ballistic, but they didn't. Hawk rolls up to the ramp, maybe two feet, and rolls down again backward. He does it again. He's supposed to go almost to the top, do a kick turn, and come back down. But Wyatt isn't up there like at practice, and Hawk panics. Wyatt sees the problem. He salutes Hawk and, pretending like it's part of the show, he marches up the ramp like a soldier and hangs out on the flat area at the top. Hawk makes another go at it. With the perfect amount of speed, he makes a run, spins around just before smashing into

Wyatt, and heads down. At the bottom, he claps for himself. The audience joins in. So great!

Miss Robyn leads a bunch of skateboarders through an obstacle course. No matter how hard we tried, we couldn't get her comfortable on a skateboard. She's wearing in-line skates and waving the Smile Academy flag. Everybody slowly weaves in and around the orange cones, as practiced. Some campers stay on for less than fifteen seconds, lose balance, and have to get started again, but they are skating safely within their limits and having a good time.

Finally, I see Odelia. She and Claire, Robbie, Elizabeth, and Joe are on their skateboards in a line, like a train. I'm supposed to be the caboose, and if I don't catch up, I'll miss grabbing Joe's outstretched hand. We push into the park until we're lined up around the volcano, facing outward. One at a time, like a wave, each camper snaps up the back end of their boards with their left toe. Then they grab it with both hands and lift it way high and down, and the wave repeats. This time, they twirl their boards. When it comes around to the beginning of the circle a final time, the campers put their boards on the ground and stomp their feet to a double beat, chanting Mighty Munchkins, Mighty Munchkins. The crowd joins in and pounds out the beat on the bleachers. Next, while skating slowly, we all fall in line behind Odelia for Follow-the-Leader. When Odelia's hands go up, our hands go up. When she wiggles her butt, we wiggle ours. When she blows kisses, we copy her. Not once do the kids get frustrated and quit. Not once do they stop grinning. The people in the bleachers hoot and holler, then stand and clap. I am so proud of the campers I temporarily forget that I need to get Odelia alone. And soon!

The campers get their big blue ribbons right away, and from their screams and shouts, you'd think they've just won a million bucks. I'm shuffled off to the back of the park where the other competitors are gathered. I make an attempt to get Odelia's attention. She sees me, and I yell, "I have to talk to you!" but I'm sure she can't hear me. No Boys Allowed has started hammering out an extremely loud beat for skate-off warm up.

Just Keep Skating

Twenty-one skaters are participating in the main event. I'm one of four girls. There's a short girl who's no older than me, and she's crouched on her board, chewing on her nails, yakking to another girl who's thirteen or fourteen. That girl is dressed in top-name skater wear. The third girl, the scariest one, is by herself. She's got on a ripped Rob Dyrdek Fantasy Factory tank top tied at the waist. On her arm, there's a drawing of the horoscope sign Libra. Is it permanent marker? Is it a tattoo?! The word **BALANCE**, with LANCE offset in green, is written in fancy letters at the bottom. She keeps slapping her board into her hand and slamming it down. Over and over. If she catches me staring, she'll probably come over and bite me. I've never seen any of these girls. Where have they been skating?

We're told to warm up, and the skaters race for the park's obstacles at the same time. The half-pipe is blocked off, and that worries me. I could have used some last-minute practice. I cruise up and down the ramps and the volcano and pull off a few tricks. I ollie up the low rail, slide down, land it with a solid THUMP.

I can't look at the crowd. I can't look for Odelia. Or for Wyatt. Or anyone else, for that matter. My mojo is pretty fragile today, and I can't lose the sketchy bit of confidence I have.

I sail over to the quarter-pipe, but a kid called J-Bone keeps jumping in front of me. I swallow the vinegar and pour on the honey. I tug his sleeve to get his attention. "You're good," I tell him. "Listen, can I get in a couple of runs alone before the whistle blows? Please?"

J-Bone steps to the side, sweeping his arms, giving me permission. "No problem," he says. Then he checks me out. "Hey, you're a girl."

At first, I'm not exactly sure what to say to that. Then it comes to me. I look him straight in the eye, say "Thank you," and skate away, smiling.

I try my rock to fakie once on the quarter and do it, no problem. I'm about to practice the rock and roll when a guy in a Lawrence County Security shirt shoos us off the pipe. This is it. The skate-off is about to begin.

The skaters are separated into three groups of seven. I'm in the last heat. Wyatt's in the first and I watch him carve around the park's obstacles as smooth as a spoon slips through melting ice cream. He ollies up the high rail, the flat bar, the manny pad, and a random bench, and completes each move without messing up. He flies down the staircase with the grace of an eagle, adds a tail grab, and lands without a hitch. Every once in a while, he throws in a front nose manual, because it's his favorite. His pop-shove-it is perfect; he adds several mandatory kick flips along with heel flips, a varial, and a 360. And he goes for the harder 5-0 grind instead of the 50-50. Of course. He is *that* good.

So is everyone else! During the second heat, a kid with a red beanie does a backside lipslide down the rail. Really? Who does that? Another boy pulls off a one-handed handstand on the coping. I feel as if I'm watching Porchtown's version of the X Games.

When I'm up, I do a couple of ollies and heel flips. I've never ollied the staircase or the hubbas before, and even though every other skater has done this, there's no way I'm adding a new move. I attack my pop-shove-it, do a 50-50 on the rail, and pull both moves off. I lock down my highest ollie so far, and start my kick flip. As if in slow motion, I feel the board rotate the full 360 degrees. In that split second, I pray my back foot catches it, my front foot sticks to it, and both feet land on it. When I realize my feet *have* landed on the deck exactly as the board's four wheels hit the concrete, I let out the breath I was holding. Kick flip, over and done. I'm sweaty, my mojo is working, and yes, I. Am. A. Girl. I have five minutes left. I can do what I came to do. It's time for the half-pipe.

While I wait for an opening, I check the audience. Odelia's there in the front row. She holds up crossed fingers and shouts, "Good luck!"

I can't get distracted. I have to erase everything out of my mind except the rock and roll. I take to the ramp like a 007 secret agent on a mission. When I drop in, I feel the adrenaline soaring through my veins. I get up the speed I need—the perfect amount of speed—and fly up the vert, leaning not too far backward and not too little forward. Once at the top—BANG! I flip my trucks over the coping and my deck lands smack dab in the middle, exactly where it should be. So far, so good. Putting any cockiness out of my brain, I shift my weight to the back and pivot like a whip, like Wyatt's taught me. When the front trucks connect, I throw my full weight—every ounce of my ninety-five pounds—on the skateboard, keeping my center of gravity toward the downside. And. I. GO!

When I'm at the bottom and my heart stops pounding in my ears, I hear, "Made of awesome! Made of awesome! Bernice is made of awesome!" I smile and wave, just as a whistle blows. The competition is over. And I'm still in one piece!

Wyatt is by the fence. I join him. I pull off my helmet, attempt to fluff my hair, and say hi. I tell him he was terrific, and he talks about who should place and who stunk.

"You did great," he tells me. "None of the other girls were as smooth as you on the half-pipe."

Wyatt motions for me sit on the ground with him. I fiddle with my shoelaces because one, my cheeks are busy changing colors, and two, I'm still so nervous around him. Seconds later, I remember to say, "Thanks." Wyatt nudges me with an elbow, and I try not to think about his arm touching mine, skin-to-skin. I feel like I should keep the conversation going, but there's nothing left to say about the competition. "How's baseball?" I blurt out.

Wyatt comes alive when he hears this question. He rattles off stats for his team and goes on and on about home runs, strikes, balls, walks, and unfair umpires. I have no idea what he's talking about, but I try not to slouch and instead, shoot for posture, poise, and even eye contact. I throw out random questions to keep him chirping along, and in the middle of it all, I realize I've nailed it. I am the Shiloh Brown of talking. I've just spent fifteen minutes in an intense conversation with the cutest skater who ever rolled into Porchtown. And I haven't mumbled, cried, or fainted. And my hair looks good.

Jeffrey Gregory is tapping his fingers into the mic, getting everybody's attention. It's hard to return to Earth. Wyatt and I stand up, and neither of us says a word as the winners are announced.

We aren't surprised to hear that the boy in the red beanie places first. Wyatt and I nod in agreement with the judges' choice. He gets a huge silver trophy, $200.00 cash, and a new deck signed by Torey Pudwill. If there are any sponsors lurking in the audience, this fourteen-year-old will get a million-dollar deal on the spot.

"Our second-place prize, and the winner of $100.00, plus a DVD collection of skateboarding documentaries goes to Wyatt Anderson." I clap like a lunatic as Wyatt thanks the judges, shakes their hands, and casually steps off the stage.

"You deserve it," I tell him. "Totally."

Wyatt pushes his hands through his wavy hair, and his bangs fall over his eyes. He peeks out at me like a sheepish little kid.

"Attention, please!" Mr. Gregory shouts. "We have added an Honorable Mention prize, a $50 gift card to Porchtown Sports. Elise and Brandon wanted a particular skater to be recognized.

Elise Winters and Brandon Richards step up to the mic. "In California towns," Brandon says, "skate parks are everywhere. They're not as common here, and I'm glad to visit rural Pennsylvania and see how a small town like Porchtown has promoted skating. I see how the kids are loving it, right kids?"

The kids go wild. The parents, not so much.

Elise says, "I've been surfing since I was eight. I understand the thrill of being on a board. We girls have to stick together to get noticed, right?"

The girls go wild. The boys, not so much.

Elise continues, "In honor of women skaters like Lizzie Armanto, Lyn-Z Adams Hawkins, and Vanessa Torres who, dare I say, have *paved* the way for girl skaters everywhere . . ." She waits for the audience to get her joke. "In honor of those pioneers of professional skateboarding, we'd like to recognize a girl who ruled the park at this event."

For a split second, I imagine Elise calling out my name.

"Courtney Lance, congratulations. Excellent moves all around, girlfriend."

The scary girl with **BALANCE** on her arm jumps up on stage. Oh, I get it now. BALANCE is a combo of what she needs to skate and her name! That's kind of cool, actually. Courtney ruins that cool when she grabs her prize, and snubs the judges by not shaking their hands. She doesn't even say thanks.

"Hunh?" I say to no one in particular.

"You were robbed," Wyatt says. "You should have won."

"No, it's okay. That's not it. I was commenting on Courtney's bad attitude," I tell him. "There's always next year for me." In my mind, I'm not sure about the next year part. Besides, what Wyatt doesn't know is that I've already won. Today has been the best day of my life.

There's a loud screech coming from the mic as Mr. Gregory takes it again. "We have one more announcement," he says. "Will the children from Smile Academy please stand?"

I can't imagine why this is happening. The campers already have their blue ribbons.

The campers stand and Mr. Gregory asks the crowd to clap for them once more, which we do. The kids come up on the stage, and Miss Robyn lingers beside them looking supermodel beautiful and extremely proud.

"I am very impressed by Smile Academy's wonderful skateboarding team, the Mighty Munchkins."

"Made of awesome!" I yell because I can't help myself.

"As owner and publisher of *Faceplant* magazine, I commend this school for its amazing summer programming, and for bringing skating into the lives of these special needs children; therefore, I'm sponsoring a scholarship program for those campers in financial need. I'll be meeting with Miss Robyn next week to iron out the details."

No one hears this last part because we're whooping it up like maniacs at the Super Bowl. This means Nellie can come back to camp!

My parents, Miss Robyn, and my mighty munchkins charge over to me.

"Bern, you were dy-no-mite," Dad says.

Mom adds, "Dy-no-mite on wheels!"

Miss Robyn takes both my hands in hers. "This has been quite a summer for Smile Academy, Bernice. None of this would be happening without you. I am so grateful for all your help."

Nellie breaks away from her mom and gives me an attack hug. I lift her off her feet, which isn't easy. She's a big bundle of fuzzy cheerleader sweater and pom-poms.

"Bernice should get an A+ in skateboarding," Nellie tells me. "Nellie Frances O'Malley and Bernice will be BFFs forever!"

"And Nellie is the best cheerleader in the world," I say. "BFFs forever."

"Nellie Frances O'Malley is a happy camper!" She wiggles out of my arms. "See you later, alligator."

"After a while, crocodile," I call.

Being a volunteer has been a terrific part of my summer. There's another part, too. A part that involves a certain across-the-street neighbor. Where. Is. Odelia? "Has anyone seen Odelia?" I ask impatiently.

Roxanne joins us, and answers. "She's next to some old lady by the stage. Hey, look! No Boys Allowed is about to play."

The crowd quickly closes in around us. I can't make it over to Odelia. No Boys Allowed starts to clang, bang, and stomp their way through their first song. I get to see them up close, and right away, I notice their grunginess—grunginess that's hidden by a photographer's interesting lighting on my poster. I wonder if Odelia has threatened to clean them up.

When the band takes a break, I leave to find Odelia, but one of the band members stops me. "You flip a skateboard like it's a paperclip," she says. "You'd be great in a music video and—"

"Thanks!" I interrupt. "Later!" I jog backwards away from her. I've got more important things to do than chat with the band.

I can't get to Odelia, who is across the park. There are too many people in my way. I jump up and down, waving my arms back and forth. "Odelia! We have to talk. NOW!"

Odelia hears me and understands. I know, because she shouts, "Serena!"

The Never-Ending Beginning

"Odelia! What the heck?!" I scream, again, running over to her. "The person who dumped me on the Baransky doorstep is—"

"None other than my godmother—"

"Serena!" we both say.

"I saw the letter that *she signed*," I say. "She explained everything. She said she couldn't take care of me? Why? Is it a trick? Is Serena my mother?"

"Ha!" Odelia scoffs. "Serena couldn't mother a baby chick. Haven't you figured it out, Bernice?"

"No! All I know is that this connects us. Somehow."

"That's an understatement," Odelia says. "Let me tell you what *I* have found out. Serena has confessed everything. Remember when I told you my mother died in childbirth?"

I nod. "Get to the point, princess!"

Odelia shakes a finger. "A poised young lady does not order another young lady around."

"I'm sorry." I put on my very best, very stuffy and proper Odelia expression. "Please forgive my unmannerly outburst. I respectfully demand that you explain the situation to me, a clueless young lady." I add a quick curtsy because, well, a curtsy was necessary.

"You are too much," Odelia says, smirking. "I like it better when you're you. Not me. The old me, anyway."

"Then tell me what's going on!"

Odelia has trouble finding the words. She's fidgeting with her skateboard wheels, spinning them in one direction, then the next. "When my mother died in childbirth, my father was so overwrought, he ignored the baby. I was very young but obviously sad and confused over my mother's death, so they told me there was no baby. And then, quite suddenly, my father died of a heart attack. Serena felt this was all too much for me to handle. She reluctantly and secretly took over the baby's care. She kept it hidden away—hidden from me, until she found wonderful people to raise my sibling—a sibling I never knew existed."

I can't budge. I'm about to finish a puzzle and put in the final piece, but a brain fart is sneaking up on me, and I'm numb. So what if I'm thinking of brain farts again. This is brain fart material here.

"Remember I told you my mother liked napping in the woods? And I used to pretend she was Sleeping Beauty? It's not *only* because my father caught her sleeping. It's because our last name is Aurora, and that's the same as Sleeping Beauty's first name. My full name is Odelia Rose Aurora."

"Aurora!" I spit out. "The letter! It says my mother's name was B. Rose Aurora."

My knees fold. The puzzle is complete. I get it now. The letter makes sense. "I am . . . I'm your mother's daughter? I'm the baby that didn't die."

Odelia takes my hand. "Yes."

I'm pretty sure the blood bound for my heart has taken a side trip to my feet. I'm cold. I'm warm. I'm speechless. Thankfully, Odelia is not speechless. She has a lot more to say.

"There's more," Odelia says.

"More?"

"You may not realize this, but I've had a troubled childhood."

I think I rolled my eyes. I didn't mean to.

"We moved here from our secluded estate in Europe because Serena wanted us to meet. She realized she made a mistake by not telling me I had family here. All these years I felt so alone, with no relatives around and no real contact with the modern world. Remember the story I told you about how my mother loved seeing me in beautiful dresses, and I was stubborn and never did what she wanted? I was her little princess, and when she died, I missed her so much that I kept a connection to her by acting like a fairy-tale princess and wearing those ridiculous gowns. Serena hoped that if I met you and became a part of your life, I'd be able to put the past in the past, and heal."

It all makes sense now. I tell Odelia, "You *have* changed a lot since we first met."

Odelia smiles. "I have changed because of you."

"Me?" I ask.

"Because of you, I see things differently."

"I see things differently, too," I say, pulling Odelia in for a hug.

I unwrap myself and sit down on my board. Not that I'd ever admit it, but I've always kind of understood Odelia's obsession with being a princess. When I was little, I felt a connection to princesses. I remember thinking that I, Bernice Baransky, would one day grow into a beautiful and charming princess. Part of me has never really given up on that.

I almost forget that Odelia is here. I take in her beautiful blonde hair, the blue eyes, that cocked left eyebrow so like my own, and it hits me. I. Have. A. Sister!

And They Lived Happily Ever After

It's the end of October, and my town is decorated in red, yellow, and orange. Mom is busy making dried flower Easter baskets to sell six months from now at the Spring Festival. Dad has been on his final fishing trip for the season and has brought home his final dead delight—a forty-three-pound striper. He got his picture in the *Porchtown Herald*. I have to eat breakfast every morning with both fish and fisherman gaping at me from the fridge. George and Ellie Baransky are not the most exciting parents on the planet, but they're mine. All mine. Serena, Odelia, and I haven't decided when to fill them in on everything. Maybe we'll wait until *they* grow up.

The skate park is still my home away from home. I rock and roll like a pro, and I've been tackling a bunch of new tricks, thanks to Wyatt. It's tailslides this week. My goal is to master them without the usual butt bruise before snow covers the park.

Middle school has taken some getting used to. My skater grunge look never made it to Porchtown Middle's hallways. Most days I wear a simple tee, clean jeans, and cute sneakers. Roxanne and Odelia about died the day I showed up in a skirt. So what if I put on an orange tee, a black belt, purple socks, and my pink ankle boots? No one needs to be too matchy-matchy. The outfit came together perfectly when I added the multi-colored jeweled barrette Odelia gave me over the summer.

I've decided not to try out for any sports teams. I may not ever be as popular as the high scorer on the girls' soccer team, but because of the fundraiser, kids know me as a skateboarder. And that's enough to earn a big chunk of cool.

Roxanne and I are still best friends. We love comparing notes about our volunteer work at Smile Academy. We couldn't give it up when the summer ended. The first thing I see when I walk in the door is a plaque near Miss Robyn's door. That plaque makes *me* smile every time I walk in the door.

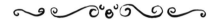

SMILE ACADEMY

would like to thank *Faceplant* magazine for sponsoring the
MADE OF AWESOME SCHOLARSHIP.
This scholarship was inspired by Bernice Baransky
and the Mighty Munchkins Skate Team.

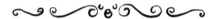

At the academy these days, we're pretending to be customers in a restaurant, ordering food, eating with the right piece of silverware, and remembering our manners. I find myself sounding like Odelia. "Sit up straight. Put your napkin on your lap. Say please and thank you. Speak in complete sentences." I sound much older than a seventh grader.

Tonight is the Autumn Dance. It's a costume party, and I'm dressed in the rosy princess gown Odelia had made for me for the prince and princess party. I have on the tulle slip that I fussed over when I wore it the first time. It's still scratchy, but I deal with it. I tug at my itchy waistline, then smooth everything in place. I hate to admit it, but this dress rocks, and I like how I look in it and how it makes me feel.

I wander around the house, sorry I got ready too soon. Wyatt isn't picking me up for another hour. He's coming as a prince, which is totally ironic. I practice walking around the kitchen in something called kitten heels—heels that aren't very high. My feet hurt and my toes are squished. These shoes are not for wimps. I wobble and gently touch the counter to keep my balance. I think back to the lesson I had with Odelia where she made me walk with a book on my head. So much has happened since that day.

I hear the backdoor open. "When will you learn to walk with grace?" Odelia asks.

We both laugh because there's a good chance I may never graduate to graceful.

"I'm glad you came over!"

"You look awesome," she says, flitting around me like a mother hen.

"Thanks to you! I'm sorry you're not allowed to go to the dance. Serena is a butthead."

"It's okay. I've got a date with the newspaper. There's an article online I must read. It's about a factory that's being built near where we used to live. We still own that land in Europe. That factory may dump chemicals in our stream, and Serena says we should go investigate."

"You can't leave me!" I say. "I need my sister."

"Our orchards, meadows, and mountains could be in trouble. I don't want our land ruined. You'd love it there. All two hundred square miles."

"Sounds like you own a country."

"Well, Bernice," Odelia says matter-of-factly. "Actually, I do." She gives me a girly punch on the arm. Then she leans in closer and whispers, "But guess what? So do you."

Wait. Wait. Just. A. Minute.

I have a COUNTRY?!

Dang!

ODELIA AND BERNICE'S GUIDE TO THE SOCIAL GRACES

LESSON 13: IT'S ALL RELATIVE

OBJECTIVE: Two sisters, who are in fact real princesses, will work together to overcome any physical, emotional, or skate park obstacle that crosses their path. (Note to selves: We are unlike anyone else at Porchtown Middle. And that suits us perfectly.)

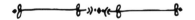

Nancy Viau soars along on a skateboard only in her dreams. In real life, she loves to ride her superfast bike, hike beautiful mountains, and travel. She is the author of the middle-grade novel *Just One Thing!* (2016 Foreword INDIES Book of the Year). Her picture books include *First Snow*, *City Street Beat*, *Storm Song*, *Look What I Can Do!* and several forthcoming titles. To learn more, please visit www.NancyViau.com.